flavors

emily sue harvey

THE
STORY PLANT

The Story Plant
The Aronica-Miller Publishing Project, LLC
P.O. Box 4331
Stamford, CT 06907

Cover design by Barbara Aronica-Buck

ISBN-13: 978-1-61188-003-8

Visit our website at www.thestoryplant.com

First Story Plant Printing: March 2011

dedication

To James McKinley Miller, "Jimmy," the male in my siblings' Three Musketeers alliance of childhood days. You are and will forever remain my precious little brother. I love you so.

To my entire family, especially those who helped shape me into who I am. To Norma Jean Miller Lindsey, my muse for "Nellie Jane." You're the best.

In memory of my grandparents Bill and Minnie West Miller.

And last but not least, Uncle Clarence Henry Miller and cousin Lamaar "Doodle-Bug" Pruitt, who definitely made my childhood, if not better, infinitely more interesting.

Heartfelt love,
Emily Sue Harvey/Susie

acknowledgments

Sadie Ann Melton is a composite of us all. She represents a fascinating collage of inner-child traits nestled deeply inside each of us, regardless of age or gender. Muses for her story include endless colorful Miller kin and friends who have influenced my life. My model for the Melton farm was my very own Miller grandparents' Spartanburg County, South Carolina farm, one that provided infinite adventures during my young years. The story is fiction, but in it, I suspect some of you will whiff tantalizing flavors of your youth. I recently visited the old farm site, only to discover it unrecognizable. Gone were the meadows and fields and wooded wonderlands. All the slopes and valleys were leveled by modern-day technology. Replacing the ancient farm house was a contemporary structure of wood siding. Nothing familiar remained. The essence of my childhood images was gouged away and disposed of. It was a profoundly sad, melancholy moment.

Then – I closed my eyes and remembered it as it had been and I realized all is not truly ever gone. Because no matter how old we get, there still remains that child inside us, just waiting for an opportunity to pop up and bestow a joyful full circle to our odyssey.

In the words of Pablo Picasso, "Youth has no age."

Hence, I give you *Flavors*.

Enjoy, reader!

prologue

Today, lounging here in my easy chair, eyes closed, with television tuned to Sirius 40s and 50s Pop Hits, I listen to a familiar old song by the Nat King Cole Trio. "Paper Moon" lulls me and trips a button deep, deep down inside me, dredging up long dormant images from the past.

Young memories.

Funny thing. Nowadays, I am challenged to remember last week's happenings. Even yesterday's. But – there's something about musings of past youth. They're perched right there on the periphery of my brain, ready-set-go to dive in. And once one gains entrance, it sends out this telepathic signal to all the others, announcing a grand reunion.

Like today.

I sigh as Jimmy Dorsey's band accompanies Helen O'Connell's vocal rendition of "Embraceable You," and my mind snatches and wraps around that bittersweet, *pivotal* 1950 summer.

The burst of memories catapults me into contemplation. This meditation stirs up a thick emotional-spectrum that gallops from ecstasy to slushing, visceral melancholy.

It makes me wonder…why has life changed so? Its seasons, in a retrospective, backward glance, do a kaleidoscopic-strobe that leaves me reeling, both physically and emotionally.

Pondering.

I prop my aching bare feet on a leather ottoman and sigh, bombarded by the swirling cerebral-smorgasbord, one flavored with infinite tastes and fragrances.

Truth be known, of all life's slices, adolescence is the most poignant. The abrupt transition from childhood – a magical time when emotions are sterling, distinct and spontaneous – to puberty (when nothing is defined and everything postured) is both brash and mystical.

One day, I was a snaggletoothed little girl who considered no question too stupid to ask, over and over, if necessary, to find out *why, what, who, where* and *how.* Never mind the endless "*Shut-ups*" along the way, or "*you ask too many questions,*" they simply did not register in my innocent quest for enlightenment.

Vanity did not yet exist. Hair bows sli-i-id slowly down my fine, stringy hair until snared by split ends. There they dangled until rescued by Mama. Dear, *dear* Mama – I still wonder if I'd have realized a bath's significance or put on a stitch beyond underwear had it not been for her, at least until my eighth or ninth year.

Somewhere between years eleven and twelve, she introduced me to Tussy deodorant. Thank *God* for good mamas.

Then came that summer. Ahhh, that magical season of new horizons. I had occasionally, all through my childhood years, been dropped off at the Melton farm for weekend visits with my Aunt Nellie Jane, who was only a year older than me. Those fun times are rock-chiseled into my recall.

But that summer was a time set apart, filled with epiphanies that divided time.

Then on its heels – seems overnight I was a young woman with squeaky clean, nightly roller-curled hair, who moved demurely amid swirls of *Prince Matchabelli* or Avon *Wild Rose* fragrances, wearing freshly pressed coordinated skirts and sweaters, snow white bobbie socks and spit-polished penny loafers.

Adolescence was angst and/or ecstasy, depending upon the moment's situation. Angst when pimples appeared and ecstasy when that cute guy in homeroom asked me for a date. It was angst when I realized it was *chemical,* that surging of hormones that agitated my emotions into goulash – and I couldn't do doo-dly squat about it, except ride it out.

The ecstasy was when that hormone-surge spit out romance.

Ah, but I digress as I sit here ruminating about all the whens. Focusing on childhood stretches that something inside me that gauges changes from then to now. Startling transformations. Makes me realize just how far I am from then.

Could it be there have actually been two of me? One then and one now?

Now casts me so far from *then* that I'm convinced a distinct time-warp thing is at play here. Why can't the two times be more *converged? Why* does my middle-age atmosphere differ so from my childhood one? Going outside now makes me sneeze, wheeze and freeze, while up until I was twelve, being outdoors was an adventure, when temperature and humidity had no bearing on *fun.*

Exploring an old hay baler at Grandpa and Grandma Melton's farm set my senses abuzz. I can close my eyes and still smell the damp earth and sweet hay and see, from three-and-a-half foot stature, the baler's rusty square trunk, whose platform struck me about chest level and instantly became my stage. I clamored aboard and – *kazaam!* – I was Jo Stafford, belting out "Shrimp Boats are Comin'" or Betty Grable, arms thrust wide, tap-dancing the length of the stage. Nearby cornstalks, rustling in summer's warm breeze, became my adoring, applauding audience.

Other times, I ventured into forest's wonderland, where a tree stump became my table, or stove, or throne. Birdsong, warbled by robin, sparrow or bluebird, harmonized to serenade me.

Ahhh, and the meadowland...I'd sprawl flat of my back on lush, watermelon-scented grass, happily chewing nectary sugarcane and watching a small plane pass slowly overhead, lulled by her drone and with 20/20 perception, sight its passengers' pinpoint heads. I just *knew*, with a child's 14k trust, that they returned my eager wave.

The cricket's *chirrupp*, the fly's *bzzzz* and the wind's every nuance tickled and teased my ears. Honeysuckled and gardenia breezes tantalized my nose. I tingled with discovery and *being*. Appetite and energy abounded. A five-cent BB Bat gave my tongue a diphthong-range of heavenly tastes. Youth's vibrancy buoyed me.

Life's flavor was sharp and tangy, *lemony*. Colors jumped and danced and shimmered, while sounds lifted me to soar and spin and fly...

To float...

Today, a half century later, I am at ease sitting here, immersed in the vibrant *when*, and I think, *I'm not so old. It's all in the mind. Heck, you're only as old as you feel.* I'm psyched out and young again. Until I move. In an instant, the illusion shatters. Like a cement Frankenstein, I shift my bifocals, turn up the television volume to catch a song's lyrics, stiffly arise and painfully shuffle to watch the neighbor's kids through my den window, romping outside on their lawn. I experience yet another piercing, *longing*, backward glance to *when*.

And, again, reality jolts.

Even though my body has betrayed me yet again and my short-term memory has gone south, *back when* zooms in like when I donned those 3D glasses at the movies and screen images leaped out at me.

My husband swears that canned pork and beans – which he once relished – don't taste the same as when he was a kid. "They don't make 'em the same anymore," he laments.

"They don't make them different," I counter. "Your taste buds just changed, is all."

That revelation leads to yet another eye-opener and it occurs to me that just like pork and beans, the atmosphere hasn't changed. Not at all.

I have.

When exactly did the change begin?

But I know.

It was during that summer.

chapter one

"Today floats upon the river of her thoughts."
Sadie Ann Melton

That summer at Grandma and Grandpa Melton's South Carolina farm would be a season from which I would thereafter mark time. The prospect of actually living there for an entire summer loomed before me like a chocolate treat. Nowadays, I would compare the indulgence to a Snickers bar. Then, it was a creamy milk chocolate Hershey's bar – simple, just like me before I acquired a taste for nuts and caramel and anything rich and gooey. That came years later.

Anyway, that spring ushered me into a far more complex world than I'd ever imagined. And considering that my imagination was quite colorful and rampant, the nuances I faced would prove to be, at times, cataclysmic. Until then, life had been dealt to me generously and kindly. In merciful increments.

Then, in late May, our live-in babysitter/housekeeper, who mainly tethered us to home's general vicinity and moved the dust around in our house, up and quit. Clodette, a friendly, robust, caramel-complected teen suddenly, on a weekend leave, ran off and got married.

With Mama and Daddy working the Carolina Cotton Mill's second shift, Clodette's elopement left my parents high and dry, seeing as how there were two Melton kids, ages four and twelve, needing supervision for at least eight out of twenty-four hours.

I was a late-bloomer and kind of small for my age. "Puny," Grandma Melton called me. "My little girl" was Mama's more sensitive reference, while Daddy saw me as "delicate." That's because most Melton females were of more sturdy stock. With my pale blonde looks and seasonal allergy afflictions ranging from coughing and sneezing to hives to dark under-eye circles that would rival football players' war-paint eye-black, poor Daddy had his job cut out keeping me from withering away.

Mama was more laid back, assuring me Daddy was just a bit neurotic about me since I'd been their only child for so long.

"Too," she would snigger gently, "he thinks you're sickly 'cause you're not hefty like Ma Melton." Actually, my beautiful Mama was a bit fluffy herself, a fact that pleased Daddy immensely. He said that when he hugged Mama, he wanted to feel some meat on her bones.

During the seasonal hay fever onslaught, my appetite would wane and I would take to musing. I never did feel fragile. Ever. I just thought it was a figment of fatherly imagination. Fortunately, these ailing episodes came rarely and sporadically, never lasting long.

Anyway, my zeal for pleasure masked those allergic spells as easily as Grandma Melton swatted a fly. I barely noticed them, so engrossed was I with life.

Everybody took me for younger. And I was quite happy with that because nobody I've ever known, before or since, enjoyed being a kid as much as Sadie Ann Melton did. My folks indulged that leaning. But Daddy was strict in another sense. His law of *do-not-get-out-of-the-yard* was nonnegotiable. Mama, being Mama, supported anything Daddy decreed, as long as it was fair. And it always was.

The farthest I slipped from our yard – when my parents were away at work – was dashing across the street to see Maveen, my favorite teenage neighbor who was always glad to see me. Rarely did I mingle with kids my own age outside of school because of Daddy's somewhat obsessive boundaries.

I didn't realize at the time how sheltered I was from mainstream mill-hill street-smarts. Not until that summer.

Fortunately, school summer break began the very week of the babysitter's exodus.

After Clodette's departure, my frantic mama lost a couple of days work before she and Daddy figured out a solution to the babysitting problem. It began with our regular Sunday afternoon visit to Grandma and Grandpa Melton's sprawling farm, where, in the front yard, the older Melton males pulled chairs into a circle and, with guitars and banjos, "made music." In another section of the country courtyard, conversation flowed undeterred.

"Ma, we'll pay you fifteen dollars a week if you'll tend to the kids for us," Daddy negotiated on that Sunday visit as we sat outside, in straight-backed, wicker-bottom kitchen chairs, littered across the grassless yard that always sported neat little dirt-grooves made by the big brush-broom. Already, my fingers itched to do the dusty duty of sweeping, a task that usually fell to Nellie Jane, my thirteen-year-old aunt.

Today, knowing my passion for this particular activity, Nellie Jane took me out behind the house to an equally bald backyard and handed me the broom, grinning shyly. Nellie Jane, with her pale blonde looks and quick, able hands with bitten-to-the-quick fingernails, was a contradiction at times. On the one hand, she was Melton through and through, stoical, detached and feisty at once. On the other, she was, at rare times, one of the most compassionate, loving females attached to the Melton name. So I knew giving me the broom was her way of showing how glad she was to see me. I took the handle and commenced sweeping that patch of dirt like it was my divine, life-and-death calling, letting her know how beholden I was for her generosity.

Soon, Nellie Jane tapped me on the shoulder, halting my frenzied labor. I squinted at her through the thick cloud of dust swirling about us. Hay fever began to itch my eyes and nostrils and I snuffled soundly, then coughed.

"Sadie," she said, rubbing her watery eyes. "You sure know how to stir up things."

I grinned and wiped my wet nose with my arm, proud that she noticed my attention to perfection. As the dust settled, I had to admit it was the prettiest sight I'd ever seen, that red clay dirt floor, with every diminutive brush indention flowing in the same direction. Even then, there was a proverbial method to my madness.

That yard was a daggum work of art.

"C'mon," she said. "Wanna help me slop the hog?"

"Yeah!" I could tell my eagerness pleased her.

We collected the slop bucket outside the back door, half full from breakfast and dinner leftovers and anything liquid to make it soupy. It was covered with a top to keep out the flies. It didn't exactly stink, but the conglomeration of foodstuff was not pleasant to the nose. We ventured down the back slope to the pig sty, wisely distanced from the house.

"Soo-ey...soo-ey," Nellie Jane called as we approached. I peered over the plank railing of the pen. A tin roof shaded the pen from the hot sun so I didn't immediately see her. I jumped when the creature swiftly arose from her corner bed of leaves and twigs, short legs propelling her bulk to the wooden trough, where Nellie Jane dumped the bucket's slushy contents.

With great ceremony, the hog began feasting noisily, slurping and smacking like no other creature I'd ever seen. This animal's energy and twitching tail and gusto for dining fascinated and engaged me beyond words. When she'd cleaned the trough, she finally looked up into my eyes. Something connected, a tiny thing. But she stood still for long moments engaging me in a wordless communiqué of greeting and good will.

"What's her name?" I asked.

"Name?" Nellie Jane frowned at me, then shrugged, looking a little shy again. "Don't have one."

"Let's name her," I suggested.

Nellie Jane shrugged again. "Okay."

"How about – Frances?"

She grinned then, a genuine amused curve of lips. "Frances? Name a pig Frances?"

"Yeah," I grinned back. "I like it. Sounds kinda – pretty."

Nellie Jane gave me a sidelong look. "I can think of lots of things to call Frances," she drawled, "but 'pretty's' not one of 'em, Sadie."

I hooked my arms over the top rail. "Hey, Frances!" I called and she looked at me again from her foliage divan. "You got a name now! Y'hear, girl?"

Frances snorted in acknowledgment, and we burst into laughter.

We returned to the front yard as, within the musical circle, uncles Gene and Tommy Lee Melton struck up their snappy version of "Dueling Banjos," while other kins' guitars rushed in and braced them up. The entire somber-faced execution was quite lively and I have to say well done. Well enough that newly-arrived visitor Cousin Ann, who was my age and just as spontaneous, broke into a little jig, a mix of tap dance and clog steps, delighting me to no end as I tried unsuccessfully to mimic her. When she finished, she and I flew into each other's arms, laughing and wildly celebrating each other. The only time we had together was during rare happenstance encounters at the farm.

I could tell Daddy and Grandma Melton had come to an agreement.

Little Joe's and my fate was sealed for months to come. Grandma couldn't turn down the then-lucrative arrangement, which would enable her to buy, on time, a brand spanking new wringer-type washing machine. This would free her from the chore of boiling clothing in outdoor wash pots, stirring with a huge wooden paddle, sweltering from open-fire heat. Not to mention back-breaking, slap-scrubbing labor over that rippled old washboard.

The very bottom line, though, was she couldn't gracefully refuse her son's desperate plea for help. After all, the family males held favor in Grandma's heart, which, at that point, troubled me not at all. Come to think of it, not much at all troubled me those early spring days.

Nellie Jane and I looked at each other, grinning, me like a possum and her more demurely tightlipped, over our good fortune. I have to say here that Nellie Jane was not, as a rule, given to any sort of open sentiment. Such display of emotion was frowned upon in the Melton clan as "flighty."

So her shy smile was, to me, like a burst of festive fireworks.

"Bye, Sadie!" Nellie Jane said, waving as we later drove off. My heart soared knowing that she was just as excited as I was. We were going to spend an entire season together, *by cracky.*

From the back seat of the ancient car, Daddy's first, a black Model-A Ford, I overheard Mama say, "I sure am glad that worked out, Joe."

No, everybody did not drive these old-model automobiles on the cusp of the fifties. It's just that Daddy had just now gotten to the place where he could afford transportation at all, and this on-its-last-leg vehicle was a deal he could not sanely refuse. It was good to have our own wheels, slow as they were, and not have to bum a ride everywhere with Daddy's older married brother Bill.

Mama leaned over to lay her dark head on Daddy's shoulder for a moment, then reached up to kiss his cheek. His head turned and I saw the adoring smile on his face and his gray eyes glimmering pleasure.

Oh, how in love they were. I knew it, felt it like I felt the warmth from our flaming open-grate fireplace at home. It spilled over onto me and Little Joe.

I must say here that my daddy, fifth down in a line of twelve Melton offspring, was not exactly a chip off the proverbial old block. Joe Melton was a handsome William Holden lookalike in those days, and he carried himself with a dignity that was as alien to the Melton clan as caviar to hominy grits.

Daddy never compared himself loftily to his male siblings, but he did rise several notches up from his meager beginnings in the years following WWII by finishing high school under the GI Bill and attending business college. Later on, in the late sixties, he carved out a decent heating and air conditioning business, one that afforded his family a nice home and a few luxuries he had not enjoyed growing up. So even back then, when Daddy was openly, tastefully affectionate with Mama, I saw a beautiful maverick that bore little resemblance to his sometimes less-ambitious male bloodline.

"I'm glad it worked out, too," he murmured, giving Mama a loving, solid peck on the lips, watching the road with one eye.

My heart leaped with joy as their love reached out and wrapped around me.

I scrooched up my shoulders in ecstasy as the old car chugged toward home.

⌘ ⌘ ⌘ ⌘ ⌘ ⌘ ⌘

Grandma Melton's was the perfect place for Mama and Daddy to drop us off for the summer, collecting us only on weekends for a fun-blasting time together. The fifteen dollars Grandma weekly earned in those days for babysitting seemed to give her a sense of autonomy. Grandma always knew exactly who she was, but that money validated her beyond the rather dismal day-to-day farm drudgery.

In those years, my mama loved a Saturday night drive-in movie better than anything in the whole world. Daddy would buy a giant cup of Pepsi Cola and we would pass it back and forth as we all munched crisp buttery popcorn. Those times in the back seat, with Little Joe and me bug-eyeing the film-of-the-night, are among my happiest.

"Come on," Daddy would tease Mama about her matinee idol Tyrone Power. "Admit it – I know you think he's handsome."

Mama would give him a long saucy look and say, "He's almost as good-looking as you, y'know that?"

That would make Daddy laugh and puff up with pride and they'd end up hugging and cuddling together in one corner of the front seat so Little Joe and I could better see the screen. It didn't matter that the windows of the car were sometimes foggy and hard to see through because of damaged, fuzzy places on them. Mama and Daddy wiped them constantly with a towel at such times to clear the view. Time with my family made me feel warm and snuggly.

Happy.

I enjoyed home.

But getting to spend the entire summer with Nellie Jane was a dream come true.

I was ecstatic, convinced that Heaven itself was floating down and settling on the Melton farm. What fun to dive into a passel of kids who looked and behaved remarkably like Ma and Pa Kettle's brood. No kid could have been happier than me at the turn of events. And when I was happy, so was my little brother.

⌘ ⌘ ⌘ ⌘ ⌘ ⌘ ⌘

Those first days on the farm were idyllic because I was the new kid perched on the kitchen bench and for a few short days, I received a small dose of preferential treatment. Mostly, it meant getting first dibs on the biscuits, sausage and gravy. On the rare occasions we had fried chicken, I was rewarded a drumstick. That celebration of me didn't last long, however, because those Melton boys had the manners of feral hogs.

After about a week, I was lucky to get a biscuit and a chicken wing. Yet, none of that deterred me from my primary passion in life. Fun.

Adventure awaited me.

The ancient four-room farmhouse, a rustic unpainted silvery-gray structure with a dilapidated tin roof, sprouted up on a rise from which everything surrounding it sloped downward, over green meadows where a milk cow and two tired-looking work mules grazed. There, I spent hours lying on my back, at peace with creation, smelling the sweet grass and wildflowers, listening to the drone of insects, gazing at the blue sky, dissecting and naming fluffy cloud shapes and daydreaming

The land-bottoms disappeared into a bordering forest, where, on one side, a crystal clear spring nestled in the corner of a rock basin. In it, minuscule crawdads darted about, entertaining me. This fountain, twice a day, replenished the Melton's two-gallon metal water buckets, hauled up the long, steep hill by sturdy Melton males.

On occasion, they would condescend to let me struggle, huffing and puffing, to carry one uphill. The thrill I got was incomparable.

Through those enchanted woods that wrapped the entire farm's boundaries flowed bubbling creeks on all sides, magical bodies of water in which to splash and play and scoop out sandy floors until water reached our waists, only to level out to ankle-depth again overnight. Oh, how clear the water. And the smell of dampness and earth and foliage was like no other.

The fecund bouquet, zested with lemon, remains with me today.

Even the barn stalls, lined up across one terrace, open-faced and intriguing, beckoned to me. One unit in particular drew me like a gnat to peaches. Straw heaped up on one side, leaving the other wall free for me to bunker down in my cherished solitude. I loved hay's sweet fragrance and would lounge there, cross-legged, head lolled back against the splintery wall, whose cracks let in sunshine to wrap me, with my imagination spinning rampant for hours on end. Sometimes reading. Always musing.

Down the hill, I could hear Frances snorting and I would venture down to her pen and talk to her. I imagined she knew exactly what I was saying. Most of the time, she would be slumbering on a freshly laid bed of leaves and foliage, at peace with life.

To this day, I remember the mystical pull of it all and experience again how I saw, felt and smelled infinite nuances of life and being.

To me, life is a huge pie, each slice a different flavor. Childhood is definitely *lemon*. Yet youth cannot completely contain it because a bit of its tanginess pops up still, a half century later. Not as often, and maybe not as strong, but during an exceptionally joyful time of love or discovery, or triumph, I *whiff* it.

That summer of my early earthly odyssey was indescribable *lemony zest*. It proved to be a quest to somehow discover the real me. A person with depth and wisdom. For nearly twelve years, that unearthing eluded me. I didn't analyze too closely. That was strange, considering I evolved into a near neurotic overachiever by my mid-teen years. Heck, during those lemon drop preteen years, I had no idea where my life was heading, nor did I particularly care. I lived in each sterling moment, savoring every sight, touch and smell of it.

"Get in here and help with the dishes." Grandma's strident decree shattered my musings as, a week and a half later, I sat staring out the window, now raised to cool down the house. The screens were natty and nailed unceremoniously to crude window frames, but they kept out the flies and mosquitoes and ushered in balmy breezes.

"Never saw a girl so flighty in all my life," Grandma muttered as she turned away and swatted an intrusive fly on the wall. I didn't really get it with Grandma, whose flavor was mostly sage-y. In retrospect, I suspect that, to her way of thinking, I was a totally alien-genetic composite dangling precariously from the stoical Melton family tree. And that's putting it kindly, out of deference to her, who was, after all, my grandma.

Being who I was, naked of ego, I told myself it was just Grandma Melton's way. That's what Mama and Daddy always said. She was not into sweet talk. Her dialogue was as plain and unadorned as her battered washboard. Her vocabulary was the same, plain enough for a moron to understand. When she meant "flighty," she said "flighty." The upside was you never misunderstood her.

The downside was I knew that day my period of grace was up.

chapter two

"Whether seventy, seventeen or seven, there is in every being's heart the love of wonder…the unfailing childlike appetite for what is next…."
Unknown

My 1950 childhood offered many worlds. But the one that shimmers still on the long-ago horizon is Grandma Melton's domain. I was at once fascinated and intimidated by my stout-framed, pale-haired, ruddy-complected grandmother. Her tightly reigned features belied the iron-sway she held over the family. There was a scruffy dignity about her, a milder version than silver screen's Ma Kettle.

Unlike Ma Kettle, however, Grandma was a stickler for cleanliness. No chickens or pigs wandered inside. Her sanitation index was, due to lack of indoor plumbing, more lax than today's standards, but considering what she worked with, she kept a tidy house.

Every day, linoleum floors were swept clean. On Fridays, they were swabbed and mopped. Before Nellie Jane left the kitchen, following meals, Grandma insisted all be left in apple pie order.

Monday was wash day. I can still smell the Octagon Soap hot water concoction as Grandma's new white washing machine agitated in the backyard. A long drop cord threaded through the window to connect it to the electrical outlet inside. Wash pots still heated the water and were toted by bucket to fill the washer and two large tin tubs chaired strategically beneath the wringer contraption that swung around from wash to rinse position. I thought of how, at home, Mama had running hot water, simplifying the entire process.

After the rinse was completed by passing each load through two large tubs of clean water and wringing out, I would sometimes help hang the clothes on the strung clothesline and the overflow loads across barbed wire fences to dry. The sheer volume of Grandma's laundry boggled my mind. Later, when she started taking in neighbors' laundry, it really overflowed. If nothing else, Grandma Melton was an entrepreneur.

Grandma Melton also had a unique form of religion. She and Grandpa didn't darken the church's doors, but on Sundays, most of the Melton offspring were spiffed up and sent off to the little country church up the road. Nellie Jane enjoyed it, and I was glad it provided her with a world outside the farm, especially during summer months when school did not afford the same luxury. The boys, until they realized they could refuse, joined her in the weekly trek. When it rained, Grandpa would deliver them to the simple white house of worship, then pick them up at twelve sharp.

Sunday was one day Grandma gave Nellie Jane a rest from helping prepare the sumptuous dinner. Usually either fried chicken or her fabulous, rich chicken and dumplings, prepared from her farm supply, appeared on the long Melton table. She would sometimes add her tasty chocolate-strawberry scratch cake to the fare. It was a unique concoction of strawberry shortcake topped with fudgy chocolate frosting. It makes my mouth water, remembering.

Sometimes, when things got particularly hairy for Grandma, a family death or her constant parade of exotic heart-fluttering physical symptoms, she would get out the huge family Bible and read. True to character, she never made a big show of it, but it was during those times of meditation that I saw an open and gentle side to her. One of faith.

Nobody actually cursed in Grandma's presence. The language may have gotten a bit peppery at times, but in Grandma's estimation, the ultimate wicked utterance was using God's name in vain.

This influence also fell upon the entire household. Her ever-evolving leanings were held in utter reverence. And her odd chest and head symptoms were borne with dignity. I never heard her truly complain. Only during her afternoon rest between dinner and supper would she sit with Grandpa in the front yard – my grandparents had the only two rocking chairs – did I hear her softly relate to her "honey" that she'd felt the chest flutters again.

Grandpa, too, respected her and loved her unconditionally. Great affection abounded between those two.

I realize in these later years just how much Grandma's strength buoyed and prepared me for the future. At that time, however, I was too into the moment to see past my turned up, freckled nose. I didn't see how hard Grandma worked at keeping clothing fresh, clean and ironed for the entire family, including me. I only saw the fun part of hanging clothes to dry in odd places and looking for the next escapade.

Soon the new washing machine novelty wore off and I was off playing somewhere on the farm by mid-morning. Nellie Jane had no such options. She shouldered the chore uncomplainingly with Grandma.

There on the farm, Grandma and Grandpa Melton's nine unmarried kids assimilated us until it was difficult to tell who was who.

"What's a four letter word that means 'got?'" Nellie Jane asked.

"Have," I replied.

Nellie Jane and I sat together, squished side-by-side in the scruffy old easy chair, working the daily newspaper crossword puzzle. Several such mismatched chairs as ours, collected from God only knew where, meandered haphazardly over the main sitting room, one that also provided a sleeping corner for our grandparents' bed. Two other rooms on either end of the dwelling—lean-tos actually—served as bedrooms that slept the remaining eleven residents. Wall-to-wall beds and cots littered the two Army barracks chambers, with mere squeeze-through walking space.

Folks were always telling Nellie Jane and me that, with our dishwater blonde hair and similar features, we passed for sisters – a fact driven home to me quite painfully that day.

"Nellie Jane!" Grandma's voice boomed from behind us as she came out of the kitchen.

Whap! Instantly, I saw stars when her big hand slapped me upside the head.

"I called you to come ten minutes ago."

I grabbed my throbbing cheek and swiveled my head to glare over my shoulder in bewilderment at Grandma Melton. "Why'd you do that?" I asked, reeling from shock.

She peered at me for a long moment until her uncertain features emptied. Then quite unapologetically, Grandma said, "I thought you was Nellie Jane."

Emotions pummeled me as I gazed at her, stricken, confused and for once, speechless.

Seeing something in my demeanor that didn't set well with her, Grandma planted both fists on ample hips and gazed down her flared nose at me.

"Would ya'll look at how she's blarin' them eyes at me – like she could run through me?" she declared to the room at large, indignant as all get out. With a rueful shake of her head, she turned on her heel and stomped to the kitchen.

Nellie Jane kept quiet as a gnat, knowing she'd barely escaped the misguided retribution. I marveled at her good fortune. For some mystical reason, Nellie Jane's luck nearly always seemed to supersede mine.

I blended too well. My identity got kicked about like a soccer ball.

The flavor of *nonentity* that day was rank pickles.

Pride? I don't remember having any sense of it when that happened. Just that it stung – both the injustice and the handprint on my cheek.

⌘⌘⌘⌘⌘⌘⌘

Spring gave way to summer and soon, the newness of change lost some of its sparkle. Yet, my sense of adventure waxed bold.

Oblivious to abject poverty, a distinct switch from my life with Mama and Daddy, I reveled amid kin-kids who were more like siblings than aunts and uncles. Nellie Jane, a full year older than me, smoothly dominated me through her sheer *adultness*.

Endless household chores stole her childhood, a fact that, years later, hit me with the impact of a double-barreled shotgun blast. Of course, at the time, I simply held in awe her *focus* and creativity at making fluffy buttermilk biscuits and mouthwatering, *lumpless* thickening milk gravy.

The thirteen-year-old soberly met responsibility head-on, disdaining my frivolity with subtle over-the-shoulder, slit-eyed regard. I pray she spent little effort resenting my freedom, since my daydreaming rapture endures to this very day.

"You'll not read the funny paper till you help with dishes," was her daily *bossy* litany after we finished our midday "dinner" as it's called in the South. The evening meal was Supper to any self-respecting Southerner. Always. Oh, how I loved to read the next episode of Dick Tracy. He and Tess had a heavy romance going, and that tweaked something vital and fizzly inside me. Something strawberry-flavored.

Nellie Jane would snatch the paper up after our grandparents read it, devour it as she ate dinner, and then ceremoniously fold it up and hide it until I obliged and dried the dishes to her satisfaction. Only then did she relinquish the treasured comic strip to me.

Grandma never came to my aid. I suppose with so many kids fighting and fussing and running wild all over the place, she just learned to turn it all off. At least when it was conducted out of her earshot.

Did Nellie Jane's highhandedness bother me?

Yes and no.

Yes, because it often deterred me from adventure. No, because she fascinated me and I came to accept her eccentric mood swings.

Nellie Jane's hissy-fits and name-calling merely heightened her mystique. "Lazy-bones" became synonymous with "Sadie." In those pre-ego days, I didn't even bother a nasty "sticks and stones" retort. I was too curious about where her passion came from. Lordy, that girl could work herself up. And in ire's wake, my wordless, *clueless* gaping would send her stalking away, muttering angrily to herself.

One thing Nellie Jane and I did together was to slop the hog Frances. We would linger a little to watch her eat. Frances' appreciation of her unsavory cuisine never failed to engage me.

The rare times Nellie Jane managed to escape the kitchen and sneak off to the woods with me were fun. Not magic, like when I played alone, but fun still. There, wrapped in the forest's pine fragrance, slowly, guiltily, she would condescend from her precipitated adult zone. I deferentially allowed her to stop at whatever level she felt comfortable with. Adolescence was her limit. I don't remember us ever romping or playing chase together.

We did word and guess-who games. Our favorite was guess-who-the-movie-star- is. We used initials and gave subtle clues and since, on the farm, *Photoplay* and *Silver Screen* magazines were cherished above all treasures, we always guessed each other's stars. Our excursions, while seated cross-legged on damp sod, eating succulent wild purple muscadines and golden scuppernongs until our tongues grew sore, were some of the few times she and I settled down to talk seriously. The mellow grape-flavor of the wild fruit always takes me right back to there and then.

And as we talked, Nellie Jane would begin to slowly, cautiously open up and once she did, she was like a sunflower on a beautiful sun-washed day

Those were times I remember, when we smiled and shared our secrets.

It was then that I saw a different side to Nellie Jane. One that loved.

One with compassion.

One which I would always love.

⌘ ⌘ ⌘ ⌘ ⌘ ⌘ ⌘

Nellie Jane figured heavily into my early education.

"There's no such thing as Santa Claus," she had declared when I was nine years old, shattering forever the magic. During one of my family's Sunday farm visits, she and I had escaped to the meadow and lounged there, chewing on sugarcane.

My mouth was hanging open from the shock of it, sugarcane forgotten.

"Nuh uh," I had protested.

"Sadie," she said, as in *how stupid can you be?* "That's the truth. Your *daddy* and your *mama* are Santa Claus." That I had held onto the illusion of a real, live, breathing St. Nicholas until the age of nine was somewhat miraculous considering how street-smart most mill hill kids were. But with Daddy's ironclad stay-in-the-yard edict, my parents had shielded me from the cold veracity that was Nellie Jane's revelation.

"But Santa Claus comes to see you," I insisted.

She humphed. "Sadie, them presents all come from your mama and Lillian and my older sisters." She looked at me kind of irritated. "Sadie, you're too old to believe in Santa Claus, anyhow. Little Joe's still a baby. That's different."

Now, three years later, she had more disclosures in store for me.

"You know where you come from, don't you?" she asked nonchalantly.

"From my mama's tummy," I replied, feeling quite proud that I had deduced such because Mama had birthed my little brother when I was old enough to notice her entire metamorphosis from start to finish. Besides, Mama had been quite open about it all, letting me feel the baby's movements after her fourth month.

"Do you know how you got there?" Nellie Jane broke a straw and stuck it in her mouth, looking off into the distance.

She had me there. "I don't know." I shrugged, at a loss.

She looked at me then, a knowing glint in her hazel eyes. "Your Daddy put it there."

My gaze narrowed on her, a thread of dread snaking through me. But the question stuck in my brain; I had to know. "How?"

She gestured then to body parts and explained in detail about mating.

Truth, bald and brutal, struck me between the eyes and shot into my bones and vitals. It was like the Santa Claus *wham* all over again.

Reeling, I felt a heavy dose of disillusionment weigh me down. I sighed and shuddered, settling down into the meadow sod, strangely depleted. Nellie Jane's words lingered, scandalizing me with details of how Mama and Daddy had made *me*.

Gross.

It was too, too much.

"You're *lying,*" I accused weakly. But by the look in her eye, one that radiated pity for my inanity, I knew that she was not.

All these years later, I still marvel that I'd not – by osmosis – gleaned from those mill village peers the low-down on the birds and bees.

At that time, I had not a clue that my innocence was slowly leaking away.

At that time, I had not a clue as to what innocence *was.*

chapter three

"Youth is like spring. An over praised season."
Samuel Butler

"How's ol' Sadie Ann?" Conrad ruffled my hair as he passed by. Again, Nellie Jane and I were going at our favorite crossword pastime, this time at the unoccupied kitchen table, perched side by side on the long bench anchored against the wall.

I looked up at him, returning his grin and feeling that unique alliance we shared.

Seventeen-year-old Conrad was my favorite uncle. Somehow, his genetics and mine were in perfect sync. He was a shorter version of my daddy. He didn't seem cut from the same stone-faced mold as some of the other Meltons, was, in fact, a soulmate to me, with his dreams of a boxing career or wrestling fame. His enthusiasm, as he spun dreams, matched my own.

He was as certain that he'd be the next Sugar Ray Robinson as I was that I'd be the silver screen's next Debbie Reynolds.

Conrad was in and out of the house during that summer. Since education was not a Melton priority – except with my daddy, who insisted that I finish high school – Conrad dropped out of school by ninth grade. His first-shift mill job enabled him to be home by mid-afternoon and have supper with the brood.

After our meal of fragrant, tender, crusty cornbread, ham, pinto beans, stewed potatoes, spring onions and cold fresh milk, Conrad said, "Let's go talk." He indicated the dirt parking lot, the only nighttime privacy setting in the helter-skelter Melton province.

We spent hours seated in Grandpa's old truck, yakking away about our aspirations while crickets chirruped and frogs croaked from nearby creek beds. The rest of the clan spread about over the front yard in straight-backed chairs, shelling peas or butter beans or breaking snap beans, depending upon the current harvest, illuminated from the light of a single bald, over-the-door light bulb. Quiet prevailed except for Grandpa Melton, puffing on his crooked, fragrant pipe, whose hair-raising ghost stories mesmerized and entertained us all, giving me delicious nightmares.

Tonight, I bypassed the stories because excitement fluttered inside me as I awaited whatever Conrad would divulge. I felt honored to be his confidante.

"I'm gonna have a boxing bout next month," he proclaimed in a pride-husked voice. "It's all set up."

"Oh, Conrad!" I clasped my hands to my flat bosom and crowed. "I can't believe it!" Conrad was a welterweight contender, short and compact – yet slender. He could have later doubled for Robert Conrad, the sixties actor. His dark blonde good looks swiveled female heads wherever he ventured. Yet he was not conceited. Never. Too much Melton reality in his blood, I suppose.

We celebrated this first leg of his dream-odyssey, he by blushing and grinning like roadkill and me with asinine giggling and lightly cuffing him on his shoulders.

Conrad was, by nature, quiet and unassuming and always kind to me. Main thing was, he never talked down to me. For a going-on-thirteen girl, that was headier than being whistled at. The only vice Conrad had was over-imbibing beer on weekends. Grandma didn't much like his stumbling in drunk in the wee hours, but she tolerated it because by the time he staggered in drunk as a skunk, it was too late to do anything about it.

Too, Conrad held a special place in Grandma's heart and affections. I never heard her scold him. I suspect it was because he made it difficult because he was so danged sweet. The only concession Grandma made was in referring to his genetic "wild hair," a term that covered any aberration from her perception of respectable behavior.

"You seen Lulu this week?" I asked Conrad that particular night, propping my bare feet on the old truck's rusty dashboard and tucking my skirt tail around my thighs. Mill Hill girls wore shorts, but Grandma Melton hated that display of female skin. She considered it shameful and the girls trashy. So Mama made sure I wore dresses and skirts while at the farm. Lulu was the cute fourteen-year-old girl up the road who spent every waking minute at Grandma's house – when Conrad was home – planted on Conrad's lap. She knew no shame in her pursuit of him, kissing and hugging him before the whole world. At least before the Melton world, making Grandma's nose lightly flare with disdain at such hot-tail wantonness. But in true Melton style, Grandma catered more to the males than the females of her household, so she held her tongue and allowed the brazen display of affection to wax bold.

That was a Melton thing, ignoring the ugly 800-pound gorilla planted right smack dab in the middle of the house. Everybody walked all around it, avoiding looking directly at it. No one acknowledged it.

It was my first close-up encounter with denial.

I knew that if it was *me* curled up on some stranger's lap, I'd get the stuffings beat out of me with the longest switch on the Melton's wild peach tree. Grandma picked and chose to whom she bestowed such amnesty. Once she settled the matter, most of the Meltons followed suit.

Personally, I liked Lulu. Being Conrad's soulmate gave me clout with her and underneath all the unbridled necking, she was a sweet, giving person. And I knew, beyond a doubt, that she really loved Conrad. A part of me, one matured beyond my age, sensed that her "looseness" was desperation to hang onto him. He usually seemed more amused by her come-ons than tempted. At least – in so many words – that's how Nellie Jane explained it to me.

The thing about Conrad was that he celebrated rather than tolerated me, as was the general regard thereabouts. How quickly my period of grace had expired. But with Conrad, I was totally okay. That was my first whiff of strawberry-flavored pleasure, a prelude to the age of teens.

Life was good.

⌘ ⌘ ⌘ ⌘ ⌘ ⌘ ⌘

Denial had it's nemesis in the Melton Domain.
Temper.
It was the total antithesis of averted gazes and silent lips and closed minds.

Since I'd rarely, in my twelve years, encountered a real display of rage, when exposed to it, I never failed to react with open-mouthed, stricken-numb dismay.

Gene, my eldest resident uncle, was freshly home from the Army. He'd been in the Korean War and was discharged because of three non-life-threatening bullet wounds. He'd enjoyed near hero status at the beginning of that summer. Brother Cletus, barely sixteen, round-faced, bulky and rather clumsy, was not, in Nellie Jane's estimation, really smart. "He's like a child," she explained rather gently. "His mind's not catching up with him, Sadie."

"Gene's throwing his weight around," she added in her knowing way, though I knew she adored Gene. "Telling Cletus what to do." She gave her head a rueful shake. "It won't do. Cletus don't take to that at all."

Cletus was normally mild-mannered, with a big old grin on his face in the worst of times. He laughed a lot. Was playful, actually. Once, when I was only five, I spent a few days on the farm during cotton-picking time. Grandma helped labor in those days and took the little ones along to play on the white, fluffy piles while the older ones picked.

Nellie Jane and I would wander from picker to picker, helping them. Adolescent Cletus called to me, "Come help me, Sadie. I'll give you a nickel." I would scuttle to help him. Then Tommy Lee would yell, "Come help me, Sadie. I'll give you six cents." And off I'd go to aid him.

Of course, cents meant absolutely nothing to five- and six-year-olds. But I wanted to please my uncles so I trotted hither and yon chasing adventure and approval.

Even then, at six, Nellie Jane seemed mildly distanced from childlike diversions and didn't join in the competition. By mid-afternoon, tired from the hot sun boiling down over the field, the two of us napped on shaded soft, cloudy beds of harvested cotton.

I can still smell cotton's clean fragrance as I drifted into slumber and feel its incomparable softness against my face and between my small fingers.

One night during that 1950 summer, when the Melton patch ran out of watermelons, the family dared Cletus to go get a couple from our neighbor's patch, across the dark woods. By now, I knew they picked Cletus because nobody else would do it.

"I'll go if Sadie'll go with me," he announced with forced bravado. I knew he was afraid of the dark. So I agreed to go with him. All the way there, his flashlight beam weaving frantically over creek bed and tree tops, Cletus sang his lungs out and whistled the spooks away. I was scared, too, but figured Cletus was more terrified than me so I ratcheted up my courage. We each quickly scooped up the spoils and returned, half-running, backtracking through the dark woods to the hungry front yard brigade in time to split open and divvy up two large melons and enjoy the still warm, red, juicy fruit.

One day, my play was interrupted by a commotion coming from the house. I ran lickety-split across the yard and burst through the front screen door. I skidded to a halt when I saw Cletus and Gene squared off, glaring at each other, hands rolled into fists. Grandma stood to one side, uneasily wary, silent.

Uh oh. Things were coming to a head.

"You don't tell me what to do," Cletus snarled, his dragon-fire breathing revved like a locomotive. He was fierce to behold. I watched as he snatched Gene's gold wrist watch from the nearby dresser, a new treasure Gene had paid hard-earned mill wages to buy, and dash it to the floor. Then with one last blast of air, Cletus crushed it beneath one huge broganed heel.

Gene gazed at him for long moments as though seeing him for the first time. Then all the fight seemed to go out of him. He appeared to wither standing there as tears filled his deep-set hazel eyes, spilled over and ran down his handsome cheeks.

It was a pathetic sight, those two brothers clashing, Cletus still panting ragged breaths, vigilant, still on attack – Gene sad and resigned. Limp. Grandma swiped tears from her ruddy plump cheeks, a rare demonstration, but held her peace. Later, Grandma would say of the incident, "One was scared and the other was glad of it." But that day, she grieved.

The flavor of that day eluded me, but I whiffed it. Felt the stink of it all about me. Yet I could not name it.

A week later, Nellie Jane, Cletus and I walked to the store to buy some candy. The trek was about three miles from the Melton place, but the day was a classically beautiful southern summer day and Cletus romped and told silly jokes all the way there. We all laughed uproariously at them and I exulted in the sheer adventure of the journey. Even Nellie Jane was open and festive.

At Brown's Country Store, we plundered the candy case display and eagerly purchased an assortment of BB Bats, Mary Janes, suckers, Brown Cows, Hershey bars and bubble gum. While Mr. Brown – peering down his bulbous nose through the thickest wire-framed specs I'd ever seen – waited on us, two other familiar teens came in. Paul and Willie Brady, whose daddy farmed nearby acreage, made their Pepsi Cola and crackers selection and trailed us out into the late afternoon heat.

Cletus and the other two teen Melton males had hired on the week before to hoe in-season beans for Mr. Brady. Cletus's earnings financed this day's country store excursion. Cletus enjoyed sharing his money with others. "Goes through his hands like branch water," Grandma always commented dryly, shaking her head.

Unwrapping candy, I inhaled wonderful banana flavor as we strolled along, our bare feet avoiding the hottest asphalt patches, taking instead to dirt shoulders. I thought of how the lovely day fit in with the smell. I stashed one Hershey bar in my skirt pocket to ensure I'd have it for later.

Nellie Jane and I licked banana and strawberry flavored BB Bats as we wound our way back down the long road to the farm. I rolled my tongue over and around the flat yellow surface, relishing incomparable taste and smell as I swallowed. At first, the male talk was sparse but civil. Nellie Jane seemed a little taken with dark-haired Willie Brady and they exchanged small talk while I watched beautiful white-faced cow heads poked through fence wire along the roadside. Theirs were the most gorgeous animal eyes I'd ever seen, second only to deer.

I wondered what they were thinking as they gazed soulfully at me.

"What's them little tags on their ears?" I asked Nellie Jane.

"That means they're gonna be slaughtered."

I thought how I ought to become a vegetarian.

"What size them brogans on your feet, Cletus? Sixteens?" Paul, the older of the Brady brothers, wisecracked then guffawed.

There was no warning.

Next thing I knew, Cletus had snatched up a stick from the road shoulder that looked, in that moment, four feet long and thick as a Texas Rattler. He drew back and swung that stick as hard as he could at Paul's skinny legs as Paul did swift, nimble leaps into the air each time it swung around.

"Aww, c'mon, Cletus," Paul tried to placate as he dodged the wildly swinging weapon, "I was just kiddin', man." To his credit, Paul's leaps and maneuvers would have rivaled any Watusi warrior on the silver screen.

Cletus, however, to my horror, got in several good whacks.

"Owww, Cletus. For God's sake," Paul screamed at the impact of wood against bone. "Stop!"

"Cletus!" Nellie Jane cried. "Stop it!" But Cletus seemed not to hear.

I stood frozen, transfixed with the savagery of it all. I dropped my BB Bat, put my hands over my ears and began to cry. Nellie Jane, too, began silently weeping. "Please – Cletus! Stop!" she shouted out over and over.

Cletus, dragon-huffing in rage, kept a'swinging. Paul, a quick study, pivoted on a backswing and began to sprint like a greyhound, catching up with the already spooked Willie. Cletus pursued for a short time, but his hulk and clumsy gait aborted the chase.

That flavor came back again, this time stronger than ever. It was horrible. Vile. Like the roadkill the buzzards ate. Cairn, Grandma Melton called it.

I began to understand that folks just shouldn't mess unkindly with Cletus because his temper-fuse was short, as was his reasoning.

We finished the journey silently. I was numb with shock as another epiphany registered. I vowed then that I would never, ever let temper rule me. And I would never tease or disrespect anyone mentally challenged. Since that day, I never have.

⌘ ⌘ ⌘ ⌘ ⌘ ⌘ ⌘

My sexual education continued when Nellie Jane took me behind the barn and whisked out some playing cards with pictures of naked adults on the back. "This," she authoritatively informed me, "is what mamas and daddies do in the bedroom with the door locked."

"*Nuh uhhh!*" I gaped bug-eyed. But there it was. Official. The death of 14k innocence at Nellie Jane's dishpan hands.

I wish that were the end of the porn cards deal. Unfortunately, nothing at Grandma's house simply ended. Accountability topped Grandma Melton's must-have totem pole. Grandma – a duty-bound disciplinarian – found the dirty playing cards under Nellie Jane's pillow. My aunt had confiscated them from the oldest Melton son's hidden stash. Of course, by gender, Gene was exempt from Grandma's wrath. Boys will be boys, after all. Thus came my first major exposure to the gender double-standard.

When confronted, did Nellie Jane take it like a woman? Well, sort of. But she just *had* to inform Grandma that I, Sadie Ann, had gawked at the sinful pictures, too. I'm sure she felt that the disclosure somehow diluted her culpability. That weekend, when my parents picked up Little Joe and me to go home, Grandma promptly informed Daddy, who promptly decided I needed the rod of correction.

That day's flavor was sour grapes. Nellie Jane took me down with her. And she didn't even get a whipping.

chapter four

"To be human is to live in a world that is filled with significant places: to be human is to have and know your place."
John Howard Payne

I don't know when I started missing my folks. Seemed one day I was happy-go-lucky, caught up in the next moment's adventure and the next, my heart dropped out the bottom of my feet.

Lordy, how I missed home. I missed the perpetual snacks of peanut butter and Ritz Crackers, colorful strawberry Kool-Aid and meals that offered alphabet soup with tiny letters swimming in it, mesmerizing me, before I added dainty oyster crackers.

At the Melton farm, crackers dissolved instantly in the hands of the kids. Peanut butter? In a blink. Snacks simply did not exist. Soup was not considered food, except in the more substantial combination of tomatoes, corn, okra, potatoes and onions, stewed together until thickened.

Most of all, I missed unconditional affection. Of feeling special. Loved. Valued.

I missed Maveen, too, my teenage neighbor who lived down the street from us in the Carolina mill village. Maveen, seventeen, was a pretty brunette in whose silvery eyes swam deep pools of emotion. They could mist over when sad and sparkle when joyful. She always had time to talk to me. She even baby-sat Little Joe and me when Mama and Daddy went out on movie dates. Those occasions of leaving my little brother and me with Maveen were rare, but I didn't mind because I loved Maveen, with her willowy frame, soft voice and childlike, unconditional love.

Like Nellie Jane, on occasion, and Conrad, Maveen treated me as an equal.

Now, I thought of her. It had been weeks since I'd seen her on our short weekend home furloughs. I was thinking of her when the lights went out at Grandma's house, just before sleep overtook me.

Arrr-arr-arr – AARRR croaked the old red rooster outside the window.

I cracked one eye. The sun wasn't all the way up, but at Grandma's house, when old Red crowed, it was wakeup time. My bed was a ragged quilt on the hard floor of the central and biggest room in the farmhouse. During the sultry hot southern season, decreed Grandma, it was cooler there. Which was true, considering the alternative was to sleep pretzeled three and four kids to a bed in the stuffy lean-to bedroom. The feather mattresses were extra hot because one sank down into them. So the pallets were a practical, cooling choice. And the change was, to me, a new adventure. Like camping out.

Grandma and Grandpa Melton camped out, after all, on occasion. About once a month or thereabouts, during clear, pleasant weather, they would sleep outside under the stars somewhere in a forest clearing. Grandpa, shoestring entrepreneur that he was, found some large abandoned wooden boxcar doors God-only-knew-where and transported them home in his old truck. He and the older boys meticulously stacked them in the secluded spot, raising it to the level just short – from my worm's eye view – of a hallowed Indian burial platform.

I never knew when Grandma and he would carry quilts and pillows to their tryst. All this was done discreetly. No one talked of it. The romantic rite was reverenced. It was only when one of the older siblings extinguished the night light that

I noted my grandparents' absence at all. The romantic ritual embedded itself in my on-the-cusp-of-adulthood psyche in the most pleasant of ways, spiraling to me strong blasts of cinnamon-strawberry flavor.

Anyway, this morning, all around me, pallets cluttered the worn linoleum floor of the main sitting room. Near my elbow lay my baby brother Little Joe, sleeping so deeply he rhythmically sipped air between his perfect little rosy lips. My sleepy gaze lolled up and over walls covered by gray wallpaper spattered with faded colorless roses.

A sagging, bedspread-draped couch flanked one corner while an equally drooping armchair hugged the next wall. Lingering in the cluttered chamber was the smoky fragrance of a big iron wood stove, now on summer furlough in the barn, along with the feather-ticked mattresses and iron bedsteads, stacked high atop dismantled iron beds, in a sometimes futile effort to deter critters from ransacking and feasting on them. Only the adult males kept their beds during the hot months.

It was exciting, the turn of season. It brought *change*. The first night of floor camping thrilled beyond measure. Following an evening outside with Grandpa's chilling ghost stories, we would bed down. When lights died, squeals and giggles erupted like frenzied popping corn.

"Shut up and go to sleep," commanded Grandma.

Then, as one, in the inky blackness of country night, everybody – save Little Joe – disappeared. At least, I thought they vanished, which was their design. Ghoulish whispers floated to me across the endless expanse of darkness as my fingers groped in every direction for human warmth. Goose-fleshed and near panic, I dared not scream. Grandma would *kill* me. My fingers closed in on a shirt sleeve and I snuggled toward it.

"You skeerd, Sadie?" whispered Little Joe.

"No." I curled toward him, adrenalin-high on pure adventure.

Arrr – arr-arr-Arr. Last night's memories poofed, I squinted through dimness to where my grandparents' bed loomed like an off-course *Titanic*, crashed catty-cornered into the room. From my pallet, I watched Grandma's ample arm snake from beneath the covers and pull a long string that stretched from the ceiling's electric light cord, then tethered to her iron bed's head-poster.

Click. Overhead light seared my eye sockets and from another corner, a four-foot cabinet radio – also connected to the string conduit – blared Farmer Gray's friendly, "First call to breakfast!" while he slurped coffee over the airwaves. I had a grasshopper's eye view of Grandpa's and Grandma's feet hitting the floor on opposite sides of their big bed.

"Get up!" Grandpa called out to everybody.

Grandpa, as you've no doubt already suspected, is secondary in the Melton hierarchy. Grandma is undeniably the family matriarch. A small wiry man with full, wavy salt-and-pepper hair perpetually covered by a battered old Fedora hat during daylight hours, Grandpa had a hawkish appearance that spoke of earlier male beauty. Farming had eroded all but a glimpse of it. He always slanted the Fedora hat brim down low over his left forehead because in his youth, whooping cough had cost him that eye.

Grandpa's profile is not as vivid as Grandma's in my later life because he was always disappearing out the door to go tend crops. Same with the stair-step order of adolescent-teen males who did not already hold cotton mill jobs: Cletus, Tommy Lee and Alton Dean.

"What day is it?" I asked Nellie Jane, who lay near me. She sat up and stretched, taking her own good time to answer me.

Mornings were not her best time. Rarely did she condescend to give me an immediate reply.

"What difference does it make what day it is, Lazy-bones? You still gotta get up," she grumped. I can still, more than a half-century later, hear her voice. It was not mean, even in name-calling irritation. It was more a weary monotone. Only when fear or injustice upset or riled her did her voice rise to high-pitch or strident. And this departure endured for only brief moments, usually dissolving into deep, silent weeping, mostly done in private.

From the radio, Farmer Gray crooned cheerfully, "A good Thursday to you. It's gonna be a warm day. Lots of sunshine."

"Today's Thursday," I said.

Nellie Jane rolled her eyes and drawled, "Oh, you are so-o *smart.*"

I didn't pay her any attention. "I'm so glad school's out and I don't have to wear shoes and I'll be in the seventh grade next year. Mr. Cogdill will be my teacher," I announced in dreamy anticipation.

Nellie Jane sniffed and cut her eyes down at me. "Ol' man Cog-leg?"

Since, in middle school, we attended the same district school, she was familiar with who he was.

"Stop calling him that. He can't help it if he limps."

"You can't wait 'cause you're gonna be his *pet,*" Nellie Jane intoned, as though it were a curse. She watched me close, pushing some obscure button deep inside me, one that stirred up something wild, that flailed about desperately denying Heaven-only–knew-what.

"Not so!" I sputtered, not sure *why* her taunt bothered me so.

"Teacher's pet," she sing-songed in her hushed way, knowing Grandma wouldn't hear her. Grandma *never* heard her.

"Stop saying that."

"S'the truth." She climbed to her feet, blasé about the whole thing.

"It's not so the truth!" I blared, nettled to the bone.

"Hush your mouthing, Sadie," called Grandma from the kitchen.

Nellie Jane sauntered away, calm and composed. I watched her go into the back bedroom and slam the door behind her. I knew she would change from her nightshirt to a dress before going to the kitchen to help Grandma with breakfast. She'd done her sponge bath the night before, a ritual I'd not yet grasped without being forced to. At home, we had indoor plumbing and a bathtub, a more simple process than the sponge bath.

Besides, at home, Mama always ran the water and made me hop in and checked to make sure I soaped up all over, then rinsed. At home, it was an adventure. Here, in Melton-land, a bath got lost somewhere between supper, ghost stories and pallets.

Why does she say those nasty things about Mr. Cogdill? Was it to make me mad? Nellie Jane did just love to make me mad. I decided then and there that she just *pretended* she didn't like Mr. Cogdill because when he was nice to her at school, she was always nice back to him. She knew I really, really liked him. He always spoke to me at school and called me by my whole name, Sadie Ann. That made me feel real good that he remembered my name all the time.

I couldn't *wait* till school started again and I could show him how smart I was and share some of my poems with him. I'd taken to writing them that past year. Mama and Daddy liked them and I suspected he would, too.

"Nellie Jane!" Grandma called. "Git in here." I could hear her knocking pots and pans around in the kitchen and smelled bacon frying. I stuck my foot up in the air and wiggled my toes. One was sore and black and blue from hitting a rock yesterday.

Soon, Grandpa and the boys would leave for the fields to work. During spring and summer months, Grandpa planted and harvested vegetables. I suddenly yearned to go off to the fields and hoe beans like the boys. I wanted to help, but Grandma said I was a curse to the cause, that I dug up more bean plants than weeds.

I was too ashamed to tell her I couldn't tell the difference.

Farmer Gray's voice grabbed my attention. "Yessiree, there'll be lots and lots of sunshine today. Ma, get out your sunbonnet."

Hot diggity! I can have fun right here. Today, I would play in the woods, all by myself, where a shady breeze always stirred, where one clearing became my beautiful castle. A big tree stump was my throne while several smaller ones seated all my subjects.

"Get up!" Grandpa repeated the order to all reclining stragglers while buckling his overall straps over his threadbare, faded work shirt.

All about me, like leaves in a soft wind, kids began stirring, stretching, yawning and trying to sit. Most of them were Grandma's and Grandpa's kids. Some folks round about there, as well as our school teachers, thought it kind of peculiar, me having aunts and uncles my own age and younger. All except Mr. Cogdill, who liked all the Meltons and never failed to show them kindness and fairness in the classroom that combined three grades and incorporated a diverse spectrum of Meltons.

"Wake up, Clarence Henry." Cousin Doodle-Bug shook my cotton-topped uncle awake. Doodle, Clarence Henry and I were all close in age. I stared at Doodle-Bug across the room sitting on his pallet, scratching his head and then his belly through a hole in his big T-shirt, one he borrowed from Conrad to sleep in. His mama, my Aunt Zelda, had visited yesterday and left Doodle at Grandma's for a couple of days.

"Your real name's Lamaar," I said to him, for no reason. He turned and looked at me real mean. *Why did I say that?* Quite honestly, I had not planned it. It just popped out. A kind of reckless flap of the tongue. Doodle's black hair was like a brush pile and his face, scowling, looked like one of those wild in-juns I'd seen in a Johnny Mack Brown film at the Saturday afternoon cowboy movie matinee. The only difference was that Doodle's face wasn't painted.

"Don't you *ever* call me Lamaar again. D'ya hear me?"

I turned my head away. Boy! He was *grouchy.*

"Y'hear me, Lazy-bones?" The sneer was in his croaky voice. *Huh!* He couldn't even make up his own name-tags; he stole Nellie Jane's. I ignored him.

Though only two months older than me, Doodle was bigger and lately had started doing mean things to me when nobody was looking, like pushing me and daring me to push him back. I didn't want to push him back and when I didn't, he made stupid faces at me and called me "Scaredy-cat."

Everybody called him Doodle-Bug because when he was a baby, he crawled backward, like the bug we poked sticks at and tried to call from his hole in the ground by chanting, "Doodle-Bug, Doodle-Bug, your house is burning up." Sometimes, the tiny insect would crawl backward up the sick, sending us into rapture.

I flipped over to the other side of my pallet, keeping my face turned so Doodle wouldn't catch me looking at him. He would make something out of it. I just *knew* he would.

All at once, I didn't want to get up. I thought of Mama and Daddy working in the cotton mill and wished they could come and see me every day at Grandma's. But they said that time didn't permit them to do that. Only on weekends did I see them.

I remember today that vivid, visceral sense of placeless-ness that snaked through me as I lay on that musty pallet, parts of me touching naked linoleum through ratty holes. I knew, even then, that the Melton farm did not own me. I belonged to my simple cotton-mill village home. There, I connected the *I am* to the *I am here.*

Oh, how I yearned for the weekend.

How fast those weekends flew – such fun times of Saturday night drive-in movies and Hershey bars and popcorn and lots of laughter. One night at our house, Little Joe, Mama and I piled up on her bed. Daddy had me and Mama laughing till we cried by sliding into one of her full-tailed skirts, rolling up his pants legs underneath and putting on her high-heels. Those spindly legs dancing a jig under that flappy skirt was the funniest sight we'd ever seen. And when Little Joe couldn't stop laughing, we all ended up in hysterics until we had to wipe away tears.

"Soon," Daddy kept saying, hugging me. "We're bound to find somebody to babysit ya'll at home." Hope would leap like flames through me each and every time.

"But Ma takes good care of you," he usually added while Mama nodded assent. Our parents unreservedly entrusted us into Grandma's care. I suppose that was wise, considering Grandma's track record with her sizeable brood was quite good until that summer.

The thing was, she literally set us loose on the farm to scatter in any and all directions we chose. Outside of a poisonous spider or snakebite or falling out of a tree and breaking one's neck, little on the Melton farm posed a real threat. I mean, it would have been difficult to drown in a creek bed of water three inches deep. In later years, I ponder and grasp, to a degree, my parents' sense of security concerning our well-being. We were, after all, well fed, passably clean, had a roof over our heads and a degree of safety.

Mama and Daddy always agreed on things. Only once did I see my parents angry with each other and then it was short and quiet, ending in a few hours. They didn't rant or toss recriminations at each other. Rather, they behaved with dignity, eventually sitting down and talking things out. Yet another of life's strawberry-vanilla lessons: the import of compromise and negotiation.

My parents' Sunday evening departure after dropping us off at the farm, always stirred within me a moment of yearning for my very own hearth and bed. My own turf. But within a twinkling, the flurry of playfulness rustling all about the rustic old farmhouse captivated me anew. Even Grandma's and Grandpa's grunts and reprimands failed to dampen my revived sense of merriment.

Home. The essence of it hit me anew and I could smell its unique fragrance, a blend of wood smoke, furniture polish that smelled like chewing gum and lingering aroma of fried potatoes smothered in onions, gingerbread baking or southern fried, country-style steak. And underlying it all was the incomparable bouquet of contentment and affection.

Of *unconditional love.*

I sighed and nestled my face against the wrinkled old quilt. It smelled of ordinary staleness. *I wish I could stay here on the floor and go back to sleep.* Everybody was up except me. They'd all taken their covers and put them away. Only my pallet littered the floor, precious space needed for traffic. I had a feeling this was not going to be such a good day.

"Lazy-bones," muttered Nellie Jane as she walked past me to the kitchen to make biscuits. More than anything I wanted to make biscuits, too. Grandma said I made too much of a mess.

Since Nellie Jane helped cook and clean, she didn't have much time to play with me. I did so want to sweep and dust, too. Grandma usually sent me outside while they did chores, saying I didn't sweep good enough or I left the bedspread wrinkled when I made her bed.

Lazy-bones. I couldn't understand why Nellie Jane called me that when nobody would *let* me work. I couldn't understand either why it annoyed her so for me to play and have fun.

I put my pallet away and moved to the lumpy, threadbare sofa, hoping I wouldn't look as lazy there. I scrunched up into a corner, curling my bare feet up under me and tucking the tail of my floppy night shirt around them. I thought about Mama and Daddy again. They couldn't come to see Little Joe and me until Saturday

Farmer Gray said it was Thursday. That meant it was two whole days before Mama and Daddy would come. I felt sad. I wanted to cry.

⌘ ⌘ ⌘ ⌘ ⌘ ⌘ ⌘

"Move over!" Nellie Jane muttered at breakfast, nudging me away from her, toward the end of the long wooden bench behind the dining table. She didn't like for me to touch her. That made it kinda hard since there were *six* of us sitting elbow to elbow. Steaming bowls of grits, eggs, milk gravy and crisp bacon were passed around and I filled my plate.

The boys sat on the long bench facing us. Grandma sat regally at one end of the table, Grandpa patiently at the other. Grandma prayed a short solemn blessing. Her "amen" was like a boxing ring bell. *It's time,* I thought, for the boys' show to begin. It was always the same. I watched, wide-eyed, astonished still as the bread-heaped platter zipped through those boys' hands so fast and the biscuits vanished so swiftly it was like magic. I sneaked a look at my grandparents. They never seemed to notice the guys' bad manners. Mama always frowned at me when I did things like that.

I listlessly ate my food as homesickness lingered, tugging and pulling at my chest. That's when I noticed Doodle-Bug watching me with this nasty little look on his face.

Uh-oh. My appetite vanished. I twisted around, scooted off the bench and disappeared outside. Warm golden sunlight kissed my skin as honeysuckle fragrance tickled my nose and I forgot Doodle. Dew drops covered grass and leaves, glistening, and the air smelled good, like after it rained. A faint watermelon flavor hovered. Carefully favoring my sore toe, I climbed the knoll, jumped a narrow gully and wandered down a slope toward the forest. Still tender from wearing shoes all winter, my bare feet avoided rocks and searched for sandy places to step.

I spotted the entrance to my castle, a large clearing over which huge oaks, pines, and elms formed an umbrella that protected me from all but the worst rainstorms. And yet, this wonderful roof allowed sunlight to filter through, making it a bright and enchanted place.

"Hello!" I called to my subjects upon entering my domain. They all bowed and called me *"Your Highness."* They laughed at the clever, funny things I said. Then I began to nicely give orders to my servants. There in my palace, my big bed had snowy white sheets and soft, downy pillows and pink satin covers that smelled like the lavender Mama used in her underwear drawer at home.

Flat stones became juicy steaks or a pie or a hamburger, or maybe, when I was really hungry, I topped it with another stone – and presto – a chocolate cake like Mama's appeared.

Everybody at my long table was polite, saying, "Please pass the rolls" and "Thank you." A big yellow butterfly floated around my head. I imagined she was a fairy. I closed my eyes tight and wished. "Oh yellow Fairy – give me a beautiful crown for my head." I spoke real proper, like in the movies. "This one is getting so worn and it's not at all shiny anymore."

Snap!

My eyes popped open at the sound. Was that a twig breaking?

Snap!

I whirled around to see what was making the noise.

Oh no! There, in *my* castle, in *my* kingdom, stood *Doodle-Bug.*

Doodle snickered like a horse, then commenced mimicking me.

"Ohhh, Fairee. Give me a bee-ooo-tiful crown for my head. This old one is so ug-gly." He scowled at me. "Course it's ugly." He sneered. "Just like you."

"You shut up, Doodle-Bug!" I shouted at him and leaped to my feet. "I'm not *ugly.*"

"Are, too." He took a step forward.

"*You're* the one's ugly," I screamed, shaking with indignation.

He walked right up to me and stuck his dirty fist in my face. "Says who? I dare you to say it again."

I opened my mouth to repeat it, but just then, my gaze focused on his fist at the end of my nose. It wasn't so much that it smelled like wet chicken feathers – it was that up close, it looked like one of Grandpa's curing hams hanging in the barn. I clamped my mouth shut.

"Go ahead," he prodded. "I double-dog dare you to say it again."

Now, that made me mad, the double-dog dare. I squeezed my fingers into fists, stiffened my spine and shrieked, "You-are-so-*u-uu-ugly,* and you stink like cairn!"

Whuuumph.

Doodle's big hands sent me sprawling backward. I landed on the hard ground, feet in the air. Against my skinny butt, the ground felt like concrete. It hurt.

Doodle sniggered, standing over me like he'd done something really important.

I sat up and shook my head, feeling kinda buzzy all over. It took me a minute to get my breath back.

"I'm gonna tell Grandma," I yelled and started bawling. He looked at me kinda funny then. Doodle didn't like to get on Grandma's bad side.

"Aww," he muttered uncertainly, hooking his thumbs in his overall pockets and shuffling his bare feet. "You're ain't hurt."

"I am, too." I scrambled to my feet and began to run. That was one thing I could do as good as Doodle-Bug – run fast.

Grandma heard me bellowing because she met me as I burst through the door. "What's wrong?" she asked, looking truly alarmed, unusual for my tough grandma.

My weeping was in earnest. "D-Doodle-Bug pushed me d-down," I sobbed and covered my face with both hands as mortification and real grief set in. "W-why does he have to be *s-so mean* to me?"

Grandma's gaze settled on Doodle, who stood stiffly a distance behind me looking for the world like Sidney Carton, the man sentenced to the guillotine that I'd seen in the movie of *A Tale of Two Cities*.

"He did, huh?" she muttered on her way out the door and to her nearby bushes.

Moments later, I heard the thrashing with a hickory stick that looked three feet long. Doodle's bawling didn't draw much sympathy from me. I was too caught up in the realization that Grandma *cared*.

And suddenly, my day turned *lemony sweet*.

chapter five

"Like young trees in a forest, her life is being choked by
climbing vines."
Sadie Ann Melton

The weekend with Mama and Daddy, chocked full of happiness, ended all too soon. The mood swing, from the high of being home to leaving, left me feeling inordinately low. Getting dropped off at the farm this time seemed like a death sentence. Nellie Jane had settled into a dismissal stance with me. Nothing I said or did impressed her. It seemed the more I tried to astound her, the more she ignored me.

Something alien was beginning to stir inside me. Something I could not label nor begin to understand. Something not sunshiny.

That morning was ripe with adventures, but my attitude grew more and more agitated. Even helping Nellie Jane slop Frances didn't lift my spirits. When eleven-year-old Clarence Henry, the youngest Melton boy, came running into the house shrieking hysterically and turning blue in the face from crying and holding his breath, Nellie Jane grabbed him, shaking him and pleading, "Stop it! Stop it this minute, Clarence Henry!"

It scared her spitless to see him turn blue. In those moments, I saw the compassionate side of her emerge.

All morning, Clarence Henry's naughtiness had peaked, from putting dead bugs in Nellie Jane's shoes to hiding Grandma's sun bonnet. Now this.

"What's going on?" Grandma appeared, wiping her work-roughened hands on her large home-sewn apron.

"The – the d-devil!" Clarence Henry bellowed, pointing out the window toward the bottoms, where the path converged with forest. Glimmering beneath the midday sun, the metal water bucket lay where he'd dropped it on the path. Since Clarence Henry was noted for mischief making, Grandma narrowed her eyes, shrewdly evaluating the situation.

She and our little gawkers' caravan accompanied him to the forest and the Arabian Nights entrance that curved sharply downward over natural root-steps, descending to the sparkling water spring. There, at the entrance, coiled lazily over a tree limb, was an enormous black snake. The "devil" flicked its tongue at us, beady eyes staring steadily, hypnotically. I shuddered violently and backed away, tripping on a protruding root.

On the way back up the hill, water in tow, Grandma used that devil-analogy to put the fear of the Lord in Clarence Henry for his ornery ways.

The edginess gripping me did not let up. My head ached and my pooched out tummy hurt. Nellie Jane seemed oblivious to my misery. "What's the matter, Lazy-bones?" she smart-alecked when I failed to rush to help her with dishes.

Perverseness sunk its claws in me and yanked me to my feet. I marched up to her and demanded, "I want to read that funny paper first."

The disbelief on her face turned to implacability. "No."

Anger rose in me like water bursting over the mill river dam. I could hear myself breathing like Puff the Magic Dragon until I felt I would explode.

"Big Tits!" I shouted, using the most offensive weapon available against her. Actually, she was just beginning to bud breasts and was extremely sensitive about it. The boys, somehow, through some mystical or demonic discernment, discovered her Achilles Heel. They proceeded to tease her. Me? I was still almost flat as Grandma's cornbread fritters. But being

Nellie Jane's sometimes confidante, I broke trust to use this offense against her.

Suddenly, Nellie Jane's hand shot out and slapped me.

Whap!

The impact was stunning. I grabbed my jaw and cut an imploring look at Grandma, who merely walked away, shaking her head at my stupidity.

I rushed out the front screen door, slamming it loudly behind me.

There on the meadow floor, I thrashed about, cried and vented my anger at life's unfairness. At my placelessness.

Where was God and Jesus? Where was that angel Daddy had shown me one night when I was too scared to go into my dark bedroom? Grandpa's ghost stories were haunting me especially bad that night and after Daddy coaxed me into the darkened room, assuring me that my very own special angel was guarding me, I snuggled down, knowing what real peace was. I felt her white wings spread over me, shielding me from darkness and evil.

But today, I didn't feel her nearby. Where was she? Where was *anybody?*

How I wanted my Mama and Daddy. Home.

⌘ ⌘ ⌘ ⌘ ⌘ ⌘ ⌘

That very week something happened to restore my sense of trust in the Creator.

Gene, the oldest live-in Melton son, came in one night with a bride on his arm.

The bride was Maveen!

My Maveen, who was my sweet neighbor.

Now, she was my *daggum aunt.*

Hot diggity! My joy knew no bounds.

"We're gonna stay here until we can get a house on the mill hill," said Gene, whose mill job qualified him for village housing but had to wait until one became vacant. Standing amid the gawkers, I tried to catch Maveen's eye amidst all the hustle of the adventure. In true Melton form, though all the kids gathered around to gape at the newcomer, the response was muted, faces all but closed. No niceties. No words of welcome.

Gene, with his dark curly hair and lankiness that matched my daddy's, was proud as punch of his bride. And he had a right to be. Maveen was a beauty. It spilled out his hazel eyes and revved up a celebratory anticipation.

Bursting at the seams to get the bride's attention, I clasped my hands behind me and bit my lip, twisting impatiently, bare feet shuffling. Finally, our gazes connected and she winked. Her eyes twinkled at seeing me and I knew that, finally, my world was turning right side up again.

Grandma's face didn't reveal what she thought of this sudden turn of events. We all knew Grandma took her time in taking to people. And we knew, too, that her tendency was to mother-hen her boys. Too, Maveen was a mill-hill girl, of the trashy variety in Grandma's opinion. So Maveen's destiny was in peril.

Poker-face set, Grandma constructed a wire, wall-to-opposite-wall, across one bedroom, on which she hung a sheet to provide a bit of privacy for the newlyweds. Of course, since most all of us slept on pallets in the main sitting room for summer's duration, Gene and Maveen had more seclusion than I'd ever imagined possible within the Melton ramparts.

The next morning, Gene whispered to Grandma that Maveen needed a wash pan of warm water, soap and a wash cloth. Wordlessly, face emptied, Grandma carried the paraphernalia to a blushing Maveen, leaving her to care to her personal needs. Nellie Jane later pulled me aside to fill me in on the details of Maveen's bleeding episode, common to new brides on their first night of marriage. Yet another lesson in life's mysteries, cinnamon-y and pungent flavored.

I didn't care about that. All I cared about was getting alone with Maveen and feeling her hugs and soaking up her words of warmth and celebration. My neediness seemed to swell as the strange edginess inside me prevailed.

"How's my Sadie," she breathed into my hair when I bear-hugged her the first chance I got to slip into her bedroom. She actually stuck pretty close to those cramped, stuffy quarters during the first days of her marriage, coming out only to take meals with the family, unless it was to scoot out the door and disappear for long walks. Those times, if Gene wasn't with her, I tagged along. Sometimes, even when he did accompany her, she called to me to join them. Maveen even went into the kitchen when meals were being prepared, but after being ignored by Grandma, she quietly gave up on helping.

She and Grandma avoided each other's eyes. I sensed it was a case of instant, full-blown hate.

"I miss home," I said sadly a couple of days after Maveen came to live there. We lounged on her bed, the only semiprivate place in the household.

Maveen's kind silvery eyes responded by misting over. "I know you do, honey." Then she pulled me to her and hugged me, fiercely. Only when my face fit into her neck's hollow and I smelled her clean, lilac scent did I realize that at least some of the dull ache inside me was from loneliness for those who tethered me to my sense of place.

"Guess what?" she whispered. I was astonished to see a tear spill over and trail down her pale cheek. She quickly swiped it away and sniffled.

"What?" I whispered back, knowing that many ears strained to hear anything she had to say. Grandma had not spoken to

Maveen unless necessity forced her to. Maveen, naturally affectionate, was shriveling before my very eyes in the apathetic environment.

"I miss home, too," she rasped as another, then another tear spilled over. I watched them trickle slowly down, over lightly freckle-spattered cheeks, then drip off her chin.

"Oh, Maveen." My mouth wobbled and I began to silently weep with her. We hugged for a long time, together in our gloom.

I felt it – the affinity. Somehow, I knew our hearts beat the same tempo just then. And I knew – though I could not articulate exactly *what* – that we were together.

In our quest for ourselves.

For our place.

⌘ ⌘ ⌘ ⌘ ⌘ ⌘ ⌘

Gene switched shifts with a friend for a week in the cotton mill. He worked the third shift and that left Maveen sleeping alone. "He's doing a favor for Earl. A couple of the guys are switching around and filling in all week. Gene drew the straw for third shift." She grimaced. "Earl's family wanted to go to Myrtle Beach for a vacation. Wouldn't that be fun?" she asked me, scrooching up her shoulders in excitement.

Unlike Nellie Jane, Maveen was not above celebrating life with me, simply for the sake of making merry. Our chat times had grown to be as precious to her as they were to me. She took to going with Nellie Jane and me to slop Frances.

"Go-olay," I muttered, transfixed, watching the feeding frenzy one day in August. "Frances is gettin' fatter and fatter."

Nellie Jane cut me a sharp glance. "She's supposed to. That's why we feed her so much."

I sighed. "Wish I wasn't so skinny."

Maveen put her arm over my shoulder. "You ain't skinny, honey. You're just – thin."

"Same difference," I groused.

"You're not so skinny anymore," Nellie Jane said. "Not like you was when you first came."

I looked down at my tummy, which did actually pooch out a little bit.

Maveen sniffed. "Anybody eatin' all this gravy and bread all the time's gonna fatten up." I heard echoes of grief in her seemingly innocent comment because she'd already declared Grandma a great cook.

"You think?" I asked, trying to shut out the sadness.

"Mm hm."

When Maveen and I were alone, during meadow or forest excursions, Maveen was her childlike self again. However, now sadness limned the frivolity. Still, I desperately took from it what I could to sustain me in those days.

Maveen could whistle like a sailor. And her whippoorwill call was eerily authentic-sounding. It sounded so wistful at times I nearly cried. I tried to mimic but could never get it right. Nellie Jane did a fair imitation, winning Maveen's and my ebullient approval.

"I'm so glad you're here, Sadie," Maveen told me more than once. Laughing together was like getting a jug of sweet iced tea in the middle of the Mojave Desert. At first, she'd kept to her room, but being Maveen, she couldn't keep that up indefinitely.

Maveen adopted an almost defiant bearing around Grandma. Just in body language. Her face remained as sweetly innocent as ever. She began to move with a peculiar boneless elegance that spoke silently that she didn't give a rat's-ass what her mother-in-law thought of her. She began to wear her loose-fitting shorts and you could practically hear gasps all about as eyes swiveled to catch Grandma's reaction.

Of course, Grandma didn't give her the pleasure of rising to the bait. The way Maveen glided about left Grandma sheathed in her icy displeasure.

We took to escaping to the meadow and forest more often. Maveen was too much a sociable being to hibernate. When around those she trusted, she became more extroverted. So now, she was openly companionable to me.

Today, the privacy was soothing and intimate as we sat pretzel-legged on Maveen's bed.

"It would be fun to get a beach tan, like Esther Williams," she said. Then she grinned like a pixie. "'Course, I wouldn't look like her cause I mostly freckle. But playing in the ocean would be fun."

I nodded vigorously. "Maybe someday you and Gene will get a chance to go to Myrtle Beach."

Her smile faded and her eyes grew troubled. "I don't know, honey. Don't −" She seemed to change her mind, closed her mouth, then smiled again. "But, shoot, who knows what's gon' happen?"

"Yep," I said. "Who knows?"

Maveen's eyes lit up. "Hey!" She took me by the shoulders. "Why don't you sleep with me while Gene's working the third shift?"

I looked at her to see if she was serious. She lifted her brow dramatically, as in *how-about-it?*

This was too good to be true. "Reckon Grandma will −"

She waved a dismissive hand. "I don't care what she thinks. You're my buddy and I want you to sleep with me. Okay? And as long as I live here with Gene, this is my little corner."

I smiled then as reality sank in. I could do something for me; Maveen said so.

"Okay."

⌘ ⌘ ⌘ ⌘ ⌘ ⌘ ⌘

Grandma didn't exactly dance a jig that I'd gone over to Maveen's camp. It was there in Grandma's subtle body language. Loud. But not clear.

Me? I took Maveen's advice and let Grandma's cool disapproval roll off me like water off a vinyl tablecloth. Strangely, when I did, I saw a flicker of respect in Nellie Jane's hazel gazes.

I began doing my sponge bath when Maveen did hers. I wasn't at all embarrassed to undress in front of her and bathe in the confines of her secluded bedroom corner, nor was she. It all seemed so natural, like when I was with Mama. And like Mama, Maveen shared her Tussy deodorant and Taboo body powder. Smelling gloriously clean, we slipped outside to the bushes with cups of water to brush our teeth, gargle and spit. Being with Maveen even made a mundane bath time warm and adventuresome.

It was wonderful sleeping next to my friend. We whispered long into the night, after the lights clicked off. I shared lots of hopes and ambitions with her. We discussed everything from boys to religion.

"Do you believe there's really a God?" Maveen whispered one night.

"Yeah, I do," I replied. "For one thing, when Mama and Daddy took me and Little Joe to the beach, y'know, down in Charleston last year? Well, when I looked at them big ol' ocean waves a'comin' up on that beach so strong, slapping at my feet and then – just stopping." I still felt the awe, the goosebumps rising all over me. "And y'know what, Maveen? That water all at once turned around and went in the opposite direction. It went right back into the sea."

"Huh," Maveen grunted.

I turned toward her and saw her eyes glistening in the dark. "Maveen, I just knew, then and there, only God could make that sea water do that. Think about it."

I saw tears glistening in her eyes. "You're right, Sadie."

It was a real special time, that night, one of many.

"You're smart, Sadie," she whispered near the end of the week. I hated for it to end. I didn't mind going back to sleeping on the hard floor so much. I just hated to leave Maveen.

"Why do you say that?" I whispered back, astounded that she found me so.

"'Cause," she paused. "You see things lots of girls your age don't see. Like the good in people." After a long pause, she snickered softly, clapped her hand over her mouth, then whispered. "Like Doddle-Bug."

"Say *what?*" I hissed.

We giggled silently, manically for long moments before harnessing ourselves in.

"Another thing," she whispered. "You know words I don't know."

"Like what?"

"Like…what's that word you used when you was talking 'bout that movie star? Uh – Bergun?"

"Ingrid Bergman?"

"Yeah. Her. You said she was so-phis-cated. I don't even know what that means."

"Sophisticated." I enunciated it. "It means classy."

"What's classy?"

"It's like – Daddy. You know how well he carries himself?" I said softly. Then I added, so as not to insult Gene, her husband, "So does Gene. Anyway, beside the other Melton guys, Gene and Daddy are classy."

"Does it mean 'uppity'?"

I really had to clamp my hand over my mouth then to stifle the laugh and not hurt Maveen's feelings. I was just discovering how delicate she was.

"Not exactly. But close enough to compare, I guess. Classy means something you're born with. Sometimes, like with Daddy and Gene, you can acquire – er, learn it. Uppity is when you think you're better'n other people. Classy means you know you're not better, but you're just as good as anybody else. Understand?"

She sighed. "I reckon. Anyway, you're really smart. So don't let it bother you when them blamed Meltons fuss at you for asking questions. They're just mad 'cause they're too stupid to know enough to ask questions."

We erupted into silent giggles again and only settled down when we heard Grandma cough and her bedsprings squeak as she tossed over in her bed.

At the same time, the revving engine of a car came to a jolting, screeching halt in the parking space outside. We tensed. Moments later, the front door clattered open and then a stumbling and a crashing sound.

"Conrad!" Grandma's stern reprimand startled me. Maveen and I listened to the clamor of Grandma and my drunken uncle as she helped him to bed in the other bedroom, dodging sleeping kids littering the floor. Our eyes glistened in the dark as we gazed at each other, picturing the scene in our minds. This happened all too often on Friday and Saturday nights, the drunken entries.

"Poor Conrad," I whispered. "He's usually so – smart. Why is he doing this? He's got so much potential."

Maveen sighed. "That means he's – able to do lots of stuff?"

"Yeah." I figured that was close enough.

"I pray that Gene never drinks."

"Daddy never has." And suddenly, I was proud beyond measure that my father was a wise man.

Maveen snickered softly and whispered, "I wonder if the ol' cow jumped the fence with Gene and Joe."

I gazed at her, not understanding.

"Never mind," she whispered.

For long moments, as the noise faded, Maveen and I lay there on our backs staring at the ceiling, senses heightened by the crisis. I felt her hand find mine and squeeze gently before releasing it. "You okay?" she whispered.

"Uh huh."

Presently, quiet settled in and I felt my eyelids droop with heaviness.

"Your head and stomachache better?" Maveen whispered before snuggling down for the last time. The unsettled feeling, accompanied by head and stomach pain, still plagued me, but for a spell here tonight, joy had overcome it all.

"It's still here. My stomach's still pooched out, too. But it don't matter now," I whispered, turning over and hugging my pillow.

I closed my eyes and smiled. "G'night, Maveen."

⌘ ⌘ ⌘ ⌘ ⌘ ⌘ ⌘

The next morning, the dull belly pain was the first thing I felt upon awakening. When I sat up to swing my legs over the side of the bed, I felt something else. Between my legs.

Wetness. I frowned and pulled up my gown, one of Maveen's, actually.

Red. Soaking my panties.

Blood!

My pulse began to pound in my head as fear iced through me.

"Maveen!" I turned and shook her shoulder. "Maveen – wake up."

Maveen's eyes popped open. Instantly, she sat up, alert to the panic in my voice. "Has somethin' happened?" she asked, then her eyes widened. "Gene? Has something happened to Gene?" Tears already filled her panic-stricken eyes.

"No," my voice warbled on the word. "Look." I pulled up the gown again and then I saw that the sheet, too, was crimson-soaked. I sniffled and a tear splashed over and trickled down my cheek. "What's wrong with me?" I whispered, gazing imploringly at Maveen to make it better.

Maveen looked at me, heart in eyes, then a tender smile tugged at the corners of her generous mouth. "Ah, honey. You're just having your period."

I blinked at her. "Period?"

"Your mama hadn't told you about it, yet?"

I shook my head. "W-what is it?"

Maveen, bless her heart, began telling me about how this made me a woman. And she said how this would later make me a mama. She reassured me that it was healthy and normal and good.

Then, in an instant, an image came to mind of the playing cards, and the pictures of men and women –

Your daddy and mama do this…your daddy makes your mama pregnant.

I gulped back the shock of the epiphany.

Maveen got up and went to the beat-up old dresser and struggled to open a stubborn drawer. From it, she took a box and a funny-looking, thin belt with two little metal clips. She explained to me what it was for and showed me how to use it.

"You change these pads every three to four hours. Just depends on how bad you bleed," she said as she pulled out several for me to use later. "I'll just put 'em here in this middle drawer for you to get when you need 'em," she said softly. "You know you're always welcome in my room, doncha Sadie?"

"Thanks, Maveen." I hugged her fiercely.

I couldn't wait to tell Nellie Jane. Somehow, I felt in my bones that this was an earth-shattering turn of events. I told her when we went to slop Frances.

Her response was, "Oh, I've been having the curse since last summer."

"The curse?" That bewildered me, cause Maveen talked like it was a blessing.

Nellie did something out of character then. She laughed and looked at me like she really cared. Like I was really equal with her. "Just joking, Sadie," she said warmly. "Only thing bad is the bellyache and maybe some headache, but it's not so bad. Just keeping clean is a bother, but it's all in being a woman."

Her matter-of-fact approach hoisted me even higher above the unsettled-ness I'd experienced lately. She even explained how Grandma told her that feeling all out of sorts just before her period was normal. And that she should not wash her hair or it would make her cramp more. Maveen overheard and added that she thought that was mostly for cold weather precaution. That getting chilled was the culprit that made the stomach hurt worse.

Even Grandma pulled me aside and asked if I needed anything – like a pad. I told her Maveen had supplied them. Her mouth tightened just a little. but I understood there was a weird connection there with her daughter-in-law. But the bottom line was that when Grandma learned of my coming to womanhood, she seemed to look at me a little differently. At least for three or four days.

I escaped to the meadow, enjoying the quiet solitude as I gazed up into blue infinity.

Womanhood.

Nellie Jane had told me that since I wasn't feeling too good, I didn't have to help with dishes. The strawberry flavor turned real, real red-ripe then.

Maybe – just maybe, things would continue to look up.

chapter six

"The deepest definition of youth is life as yet untouched by tragedy."
Alfred North Whitehead

The day offered no warning.

Things had settled back into routine after my womanhood initiation. I didn't feel so different after the menses ceased that week. What I did feel were subtle changes in the dynamics between the Melton females.

I didn't have long to mull over them, however. Fate had other ideas.

Gene had returned to his regular second-shift job, reclaiming his bed space beside Maveen. I was again sleeping on the floor-pallet beside my little brother. The new spiritual connection between Maveen and me galvanized. She began to open up and share her disappointments with me. These divulgences came mostly during our long walks over the farm's meadows and forest.

"Gene won't tell his Ma to treat me better," she said that day, a bit testily as we spaced ourselves further from the house by exploring the bottoms. "I don't know why she don't like me, but I don't really care anymore." She tossed her head while flipping a stone with her sandaled foot. I thought she looked prettier than ever when her temper sparked, a rare occurrence. She looked a lot like the tragic young actress, Millie Perkins, in those days, with an elfin shape to her face and features. Thin, too. Almost skinny but looked wonderful in her clothes. She rarely raised her voice, but her soft words let others know she didn't put up with any crap.

Not even from Grandma Melton.

Maveen, though gentle and loving, had a side to her that was as stubborn as my Grandma's. Therein lay the crux.

"I wish she'd treat you better," I said. "She's just kinda strange sometimes, Maveen. It's not you. She's that way with others, too. Even me, at times."

Maveen snorted delicately and paused to look at me. "Honey, *it is* me, too. She hates my guts 'cause I married her boy. She's plain jealous is what's wrong with her."

"You think?"

"I know." She started walking again.

"I'm sorry," I muttered, trailing along, wanting to console her but feeling helpless to do so. Her stance was unbending.

"It's not your fault."

Nellie Jane, strangely, did not seem to resent my time with Maveen. I sensed that underneath the stoical silence, my aunt really liked Maveen. She demonstrated this in little things she did when Grandma wasn't looking. Like saving Maveen an extra serving of apple cobbler, with fresh cream, her favorite dessert. And sneaking it into her room so it could be eaten in privacy. And several times, when she could manage to finish her chores quickly, Nellie Jane tagged along on our walks, adding warmly to conversations. Most importantly, she did not go tattle when Maveen vented her mother-in-law frustrations. And I knew that Maveen, being Maveen, loved Nellie Jane. She listened to her entirely, with no reservations or preconceived concepts of who this paradoxical person really was.

One day, in an entirely offbeat mode, Nellie Jane referred to Buck Swaney, a bucktoothed, unethical slouch she couldn't stand. "He's ugly as skunk cabbage and if you yawn, he could steal the chew o' tobacco outta your mouth," she swore solemnly, cracking both of us up at the brief, razor-honed summary.

Then Nellie Jane gifted us with one of her rare, genuine grins of delight. And I knew then she loved Maveen.

Maveen had won over the entire clan. All except Grandma.

In the past week, comic strips began to appear beside my dinner plate without my asking. In turn, I helped with dishes without being told.

But on that Saturday night, the uneasy peace exploded into smithereens.

Grandma had just turned off the lights and our pallets littered the floor when bright lights and a wailing siren shattered the quiet. Like a store shelf of Jack-in-the-boxes, mussed heads popped up in the dark. We sat there, sleep woozy, staring bug-eyed at wild white light streaking around the old door's crease and spilling through the narrow windows. A loud rap on the front door brought us to our bare feet and Grandpa, pulling his overalls on quickly, to the door.

Cautiously, he opened it and peered out, squinting against the blinding lights. "What you want?"

Silhouetted in the headlights of two police cars, an officer said, "Mr. Melton?"

Grandma now hovered tensely behind him, her loose cotton, home-sewn gown billowing around her ankles.

"Yeah?" Grandpa croaked.

"You have a son named Conrad Melton?"

Grandma stepped around him. "What's wrong?" her voice faltered. I heard both wavering courage and dread.

"I'm sorry, Mrs. Melton." The officer's voice was soft, kind. "Your son was in a head-on collision on Highway 290. He was pronounced dead at the scene."

"Oh, my God," I felt my knees turn to water as I sank to the floor, my face buried in my hands. I heard the bedroom door squeak open as Gene and Maveen crept in and I felt Maveen's arms slide around me as she dropped beside me on the floor.

But it was that one heart-rending scream from Grandma that I remember most about that night.

Life there would never again be the same.

⌘ ⌘ ⌘ ⌘ ⌘ ⌘ ⌘

The next three days passed in a blur. Daddy and Mama came and helped take care of Grandma, Grandpa and the rest of us. The Methodist church and Church of Christ, both in the rural area, took care of feeding the huge clan. Neighbors and kin came and went, some dropping off cakes or Pepsi Colas or fried chicken or cold cut platters from the Beacon Drive-in in Spartanburg.

"He was playing 'Chicken' with Johnny Mack Mason," swollen-eyed Nellie Jane explained to me. Her hoarse voice shook and her words quavered.

"Everybody loved him," I reminded her, taking both her cold hands in mine to warm and encourage, expecting her to maybe reject such intimate succor or grow uncomfortable. But she did neither. Instead, her generous lips curved ever so slightly into a grateful, wobbly smile. "Nobody has said anything bad about him."

Which was absolutely true.

Despite Conrad's terrible fate, everybody loved him. He was one of those rare creatures who glowed with a quiet, non-intrusive charisma and had so much to offer had he only made wiser decisions.

Sadly, that unmerited favor meant little in the face of things. It made the entire situation infinitely more tragic. Even the other driver in the head-on crash miraculously survived with serious yet not life-threatening injuries. Only person Conrad hurt was himself. He was his own worst enemy. His weekend binge-drinking persona was a gross departure from the pleasant Conrad I knew.

After that initial emotional outburst from Grandma, hers and Grandpa's display of grief was limited to an eerie stoical silence and discreet swiping away of tears. It was the look in my grandmother's eyes that struck me like a cold, steel mallet. The anguish in those hazel depths was stark and primitive. That look drove home that Conrad had been Grandma's heart. Her soft spot.

As he had been mine. His beauty and potential was sabotaged by alcohol abuse. The heartbreak of it sunk its claws into me and would not turn loose. Nellie Jane and I wept together in the meadow, where no one reviewed our display.

As we huddled together there in the sweet honeysuckled breezes, beneath a derisive sun, Clarence Henry appeared and plopped down beside us. The eleven-year-old mischief-maker bawled like an agitated newborn, until his breath ran out and his face turned blue and Nellie Jane, putting aside her own grief, grabbed his shoulders, shook him and cried, "Stop it! Stop it right now!" When he gasped in some air and pink returned, she gathered him in her arms and held him until he was restored.

Conrad's body was brought home, his casket set up in the main sitting room. To make space for it, most furniture was piled into one of the lean-to bedrooms. It didn't matter about sleeping space; nobody slept much, and when we did, it was slouched down in any armed chair or on the floor, tucked into a corner to catch a few winks.

The aptly named wake did, indeed, honor my Uncle Conrad.

It was hard to gaze upon his beauty. Make-up covered some of it, to camouflage injuries, but – in his youth – he was still breathtaking. The loss was so profound it smothered me. I had to turn away, gasping for breath. I felt I would die from it. I no longer had my Melton-male soul mate. How could this happen to someone so young and vital – so *alive?*

With so many unfulfilled dreams?

Lulu, his girlfriend, was inconsolable. Her wails could be heard all over the countryside that first day and into the next night. When Lulu, beside herself and debilitated with grief, was half-carried into the house to view Conrad, Grandma Melton actually went to her and put her arms around her briefly, silently validating her sorrow.

I wept, along with everyone present who witnessed the profound moment.

To her credit, Maveen tried to comfort Grandma. I watched her overtures be ignored or rebuffed and experienced a different grief. I watched Maveen wither under the rejection. I watched hope die. I watched her walk away. Empty. I decided then and there that I would never, ever cause anyone that kind of pain. I promised the Maker that I would have a forgiving and merciful heart. After all, it doesn't cost anything to be kind, does it?

Mama and Daddy, knowing how I'd loved Conrad, gave special attention to being with me. Daddy's strong, gentle hands and rumbling voice consoled and soothed me while Mama's arms held me close as she murmured how much she loved me and how it would be all right.

Conrad was laid to rest in a lone burial plot in the little country church cemetery where generations of Meltons lay. No wife or child would rest next to him. Ever.

It broke my heart yet again.

When the last flowers were placed over the fresh dirt mound, I felt like I had been wrung out like a dish rag.

Nellie Jane and I slopped Frances that night. Frances's appetite, unlike ours, remained unaffected. It seemed surreal as I stood there, witnessing a creature's zesty *being.*

I burst into tears and presently heard Nellie Jane weeping, too.

Would it ever stop hurting?

⌘ ⌘ ⌘ ⌘ ⌘ ⌘ ⌘

Life goes on. Another of life's lessons.

No one is indispensable. The world does not stop when someone young dies. Normalcy returns with cruel efficiency. The flavor was dark and bitter, yet reeked of carnations and funeral flowers, a smell that smothers me till this very day.

It appalled me, the way life ignored Conrad's demise. But the relentlessness of life's continuity superseded my indignation and soon, it overrode even my frame of mind.

Grandma and Grandpa never again talked openly about Conrad. They probably talked about him in private, but not for other ears to hear. I would catch Grandma wiping her eyes with her apron when she thought no one was looking and I knew she was thinking about him. Grandpa's departures to the fields were ghostly silent.

The younger kids' activities in those following days and weeks were dissonantly solitary and subdued. Laughter was silenced. Nellie Jane spent more time with Maveen and me when we escaped to the meadow or forest to have girl talk.

"I rolled up a blanket for us to sit on," Nellie Jane said, revealing a threadbare blanket, rolled up discreetly under her arm, to spread for our seat. She didn't say it, but she didn't want to make too big a production of our outings for fear that Grandma would disapprove. Fun was *so not* a priority with my grandmother. Was, when it came to Nellie Jane, Maveen and me, frivolous. But now that the entire house lay thick with death's pall, her inclination to vigilance waned.

That was one of the rare times I saw in my stoical grandma *vulnerability.*

So the three younger Melton females spent more time lolling indolently on earth's floor, inhaling the distinctive fragrance of earth, creek bed and foliage. We shared things about Conrad that made us laugh and some that made us cry. But the important thing was that we kept him *alive* for a while longer. To me, that was somehow the most important thing on earth. To not forget my soulmate, Conrad. The commiserations were infinitely precious because we three female Meltons were on the same page in mind, soul and body as we lay there together, remembering.

And in a strange way, for once, we were on the same page as Grandma.

My weekend home furlough helped me begin to heal. Being with Mama and Daddy and seeing Debbie Reynolds in *I Love Melvin* at the King Cotton Drive-In Theater buoyed me from the low-hanging pall. "Abba Dabba Honeymoon," despite my vow to honor Conrad's departure, soon had my toes tapping, my lips syncing and my brain computing the lyrics. Even Little Joe joined in with me as I accompanied Debbie, with Mama and Daddy harmonizing a little, too.

We ended up belly-laughing at all the screw-ups.

It felt good.

⌘ ⌘ ⌘ ⌘ ⌘ ⌘ ⌘

Few things overcome grief, but new life has a tendency to do just that.

It was a joyful event when Daisy, the Meltons' Heinz 57 female gave birth to puppies. The mama-dog, who'd wandered onto the farm one day and blended into the household in a remarkable way, considering the family's usual slow adaptation to new critters. Daisy seemed to smile at me and Nellie Jane when we went to the barn where she'd given birth and now nested. We dropped to our knees to pick up and nuzzle the squiggly, joyful little bundles of multi-tan fuzz.

We ran to get Maveen and share our discovery with her. She was as enthralled as we were. For the next few weeks, we watched the metamorphosis of the pups. One, in particular, was my favorite. Flossie's exuberant celebration of me made me tingle with joy. I even snuck her into Maveen's corner several times to feed her crumbs and leftovers. That lasted until Grandma found out and warned me not to get "too attached."

"Why should it be bad to love a puppy?" I asked Maveen after I'd taken Flossie back outside to join the rest of the litter, who now wandered freely about the yard, romping and joining in the kids' play.

"Huh. She don't believe in that kinda thing. It's too much fun," Maveen drawled. "So it's bad."

One day, Nellie Jane joined Maveen and me at the meadow. She was pale and shaking. When I asked her what was wrong, she looked at me with stricken eyes.

"Da's gonna kill 'em."

"Who?" Maveen asked, suddenly concerned. My hair stood on end and dread coursed through my veins. I knew it was going to be something I really, really did not want to know.

"Ma saw Daisy sucking eggs. And the puppies, too." Nellie Jane looked down at her hands as they grasped meadow grass and yanked them up with loud *pings*. "At our house, that's a death sentence."

"Why?" I wailed, horrified.

Nellie Jane slowly shook her head and looked away. "'Cause, once they taste eggs, they won't ever stop. Ma says the eggs are more important." I heard the acceptance in her voice, saw it on her face. Resignation.

I jumped to my feet and began running, tears coursing down my cheeks.

"Flossie!" I shrieked, willing my legs to move faster.

Boom!

The first shotgun blast. Oh God. Let me find Flossie.

Boom!

I could see Grandpa in the yard, shotgun anchored on his skinny shoulder, drawing a bead on another target.

Boom!

Before him lay two lifeless, fluffy forms. A third was flopping about in death throes.

Oh God! I froze. Flossie, at the edge of the yard, saw me and began to wag her tail exuberantly, a smile on her little face.

Boom! I watched in horror as my little pet was blown apart and began to twitch and wallow, dying.

I could not bear it. I could not! *Oh God, ohGodohGod! Not little Flossie!*

I ran to the yard, past Grandma, who sat stoically watching the drama. Past Grandpa, the killer, and disappeared into the house to Maveen's sanctuary. I dove onto her bed, usually my safe haven in the dwelling.

Not today.

Boom!....Boom….Boom.

I burrowed my head under the pillow, clawing it, every atom of my body constricting with shock and loathing.

Eaten alive with the sheer horror of it all.

Presently, I felt Maveen's hands rub my arm, soothe my back.

"I hate it!" I moaned. "I hate it, hate it, *hate it!*"

"Me, too," Maveen murmured hoarsely. Her bedroom corner's tiny makeshift window provided the only view to the front yard and I knew she'd witnessed at least the first of the slaughter.

Silence. But even it screamed and tore at me.

I cautiously removed the old musty pillow from my head and, clamoring up on my knees, peered outside. Six lifeless furry puddles littered the yard amid pools of blood. I immediately plopped backward on the bed, moaning, feeling my own life's blood leaving my head. It was too, too much. I felt sick to my stomach and my hands tingled.

Nellie Jane soon crept in and crawled up on the bed with us. I could tell she was nearly as stunned as we were. Almost. She was just a little more seasoned than we were to life's brutality.

"Ya'll know that they don't want to kill 'em," she shrugged sadly with acceptance. "It's just that we need them eggs. Once the dogs eat 'em, they can't be broke from it."

A part of me understood. But I still could not come to grips with putting eggs above a life. In this case, six little lives.

The front screen door slammed. Grandma summoned Nellie Jane to help cook supper. Again, life went on.

After Nellie Jane left, Maveen and I lolled there, silent and grieving, until suppertime. Trying to make sense of the carnage that lay just beyond the bedroom wall.

⌘ ⌘ ⌘ ⌘ ⌘ ⌘ ⌘

Mama consoled me that weekend. "They're just different," she said of my grandparents. "They're good people. Things are different when you have to raise your own food. They don't earn weekly wages like Daddy and I do. We can just go out and buy what we need. But they can't. It's cruel to have to live that way. And," she smiled sympathetically and gently pushed back my too-long bangs, "I understand how you feel, honey. You've got a real tender heart." Then she sighed. "Too tender sometimes."

I was just now getting back my appetite. I'd not eaten much for the past two days. I missed my little Flossie. Missed her warmth and velvety tongue licking my face – the *life* *in* her. We, Nellie Jane, Maveen, Clarence Henry and I, had buried her, along with the other five pitiful bodies, deep in the woods. The activity of collecting hoes and shovels from the barn, digging the small graves, wrapping the still bundles in burlap we'd found in the barn and burying them all with some modicum of dignity seemed to mystically begin our healing.

"Let's sing something," Clarence Henry suggested, surprising us all.

We sang "Amazing Grace." Then we recited the Lord's Prayer and even did the Pledge of Allegiance for good measure. We gathered some wildflowers from the meadow as a finishing touch to the earthen mounds, now covered with forest mulch and bordered with creek-smoothed stones. The fecund fragrance of that scene and the reverence for those little sacrificed lives remains with me even now.

"It was pretty," I murmured today as Mama and I lingered at the dinner table. Daddy had gone out into our front yard with Little Joe to watch him ride his tricycle. Knowing the Melton clan's propensity for destroying anything mechanical, Daddy and Mama kept the trike at home for Little Joe's weekend enjoyment.

"What?" she asked, sipping her coffee.

"The graveyard. We're gonna get some big rocks and make six tombstones inside that plot of graves."

"That's sweet, honey."

Mama always understood.

How I missed living at home.

In my very own place.

⌘⌘⌘⌘⌘⌘⌘

Then, when I got back to the farm, I could not find Maveen.

"She's not here," Nellie Jane grabbed my hand when I rushed to Maveen's room.

"Where is she?" An unrest seized me. A black, thick, sticky dread.

"This morning, she told Gene she was leaving till he got them a village house," Nellie Jane whispered to me upon my arrival that Sunday evening, just before sundown.

"Where'd she go?" The words came out squeaky, weak.

"To her mama's."

"I didn't see her."

Nellie Jane pulled me outside and down to the barn where we could talk in private. We entered my favorite stall where a sweet-smelling hay-carpet welcomed us to sit.

"So she's gone," I muttered inanely, feeling my heart sink out the bottom of my feet. How was I going to make it without Maveen? Nellie Jane looked at me with compassion, and I knew that she, too, would miss Maveen.

"What's Gene saying?" I asked, curious.

She shrugged. "He was mad at Maveen at first, but now he's moping around real bad. Ma tells him that he's actin' like an addled rooster. That she knew all along how flighty Maveen was. Gene don't like Ma to talk like that. He told her to quit bad-mouthing his wife."

I stared at her, mouth open. "He said that to Grandma?"

Nellie Jane looked at me with her heart in her eyes. "He shoulda been that way 'fore Maveen got a gut-full and left."

"Yeah," I muttered, releasing a long, ragged sigh, thinking how things can change so fast.

⌘⌘⌘⌘⌘⌘⌘

That week seemed the longest ever. By the weekend, I felt I would die from Maveen's absence. When Mama and Daddy finally collected my brother and me and drove us home, I asked permission and dashed across the street to Maveen's mother's house.

Maveen met me at the door and engulfed me in a bear hug and I realized she must have been watching for my arrival home. It made my heart float like a helium balloon. Made me feel really, really special and treasured. Because I knew her heart was breaking.

Later that evening, Mama and Daddy, perhaps seeing how happy I was to see Maveen and knowing she needed a diversion, asked her to babysit Little Joe and me and they would go out on a real date. This evening, the arrangement was extra-special poignant for me, after having pined all week for my friend.

We turned on the radio and tuned in a station that played pop songs, the kind of big band sounds that Maveen and I both liked. Tonight featured Cole Porter favorites. Ella Fitzgerald's "Let's Fall in Love" sent me into dreamy ecstasy as we pondered what we wanted to do with the evening.

Maveen's huge gray eyes looked deeper and sadder than I'd ever seen them, but she was doing her best to keep up her spirit for my sake. "You don't have to be happy," I told her and hugged her again. "I know you're hurting over Gene."

"Yeah." She attempted a smile but came real short of it. Tears rushed to her eyes. "I miss 'im, Sadie." She snuffled and then thrust out her chin and forced a real smile. "But I'll live. Thing is to keep busy. Taking care o' Mama keeps me hopping all day. It's the nights that are the hardest."

"We'll make these hours go by, fast and fun," I said hopefully.

"Hey! I know," she said, suddenly brightening. "Let's bake a cake."

Little Joe, an early-to-bedder, was already fast asleep and tucked in. "I've got a cake recipe you'll love," Maveen said, picking up steam a bit. "Especially the buttercream frosting." She knew of my sweet-tooth and she was a wonderful cook. Learned from her mama. "And best of all, it's easy. You can do most of it. How about that?" She grinned at me, like *I dare you.*

"Huh. I can do it." After all, I'd watched Nellie Jane and Grandma stir up desserts all summer, everything from Apple Cobbler to Strawberry-Chocolate Cake. And I knew that deep down, Maveen sensed how desperately I wanted to cook at Grandma's house. She, too, had been shut out of Grandma's inner sanctum. She also knew that the rejection dug in and resided someplace deep inside me.

We gathered the ingredients for a simple yellow scratch cake and the icing. Mama had most of the items and Maveen dashed across to her mother's house and plundered cabinets until she found the ones we lacked.

Soon, the strains of selections like Ella Fitzgerald singing "Night and Day" and Bing Crosby crooning "Don't Fence Me In" had Maveen and me warbling along with the lyrics, absolutely rhapsodized since we'd both seen the 1945 movie *Night and Day,* the story of Cole Porter's life, starring Cary Grant and Alexis Smith. Forever after, when I heard Porter tunes, I would picture a resplendent Cary Grant sitting at the piano, playing and singing. Never mind the gross discrepancies between the story's truth and fiction; I would ever more see Cary's arms held out to Alexis, standing on his own once more at movie's end, and her running into them with tears sparkling and flashing like Technicolor diamonds in her beautiful eyes.

Scraping the batter bowl and depositing the last drippings into one of three greased, floured pans, I licked the spoon clean and declared, "I love Cole Porter songs, Maveen."

"Me, too," she agreed and sighed as she rinsed out the bowl to use it to later mix butter, powdered sugar and rich cream for the buttercream frosting. She'd insisted I do all the actual mixing and baking. "That way, it's your cake. You can say you done it all by yourself."

"I miss my pretty music when I'm not home," I said as I washed the mixer blades. Mama had bought an electric mixer just this year. "I'm glad I don't have to do the old manual mixer anymore. I used to beat the egg whites for meringue for Mama. Took fore-ver. This is more fun."

"Yeah," Maveen agreed as she rinsed the blades and dried them. "I like Webb Pierce's 'Satisfied Mind.' Some country music's okay. It's just that when that's all you ever hear, it gets kinda – old."

"Gotta run pee," Maveen said and dashed to the bathroom, located on the back porch. When she finished, she came in grinning. "At least I don't have to go to the barn privy now."

I rolled my eyes as I arranged the measuring tools and told her about the peeping incident the week before, shocking Maveen completely. I felt somewhat vindicated at her response and support. I started measuring butter and confectioner's sugar as Porter's "I Get a Kick Out of You" struck up. Maveen and I both swooned and swayed with the catchy song, one that plucked at our heartstrings and pulled out the romantic in us.

We took time out for the layers to bake for twenty-five to thirty minutes.

Lounging on Mama's blue sofa, we propped bare feet up on the living room coffee table and chatted a while about Maveen's mama's health problems and how that now she was home, Maveen could look after her. We talked briefly about Gene and how she knew that he loved her but that Grandma didn't like her and made it miserable for her to live there. So, Gene would either find out he could not live without Maveen or it would be over.

Tears pooled in her deep, soulful eyes. "I don't feel like I can live without 'im," she murmured brokenly. "But he's gotta choose, Sadie. I can't live there anymore. It'll kill me."

"I know." And I did. It didn't make it any easier for me, though, being there without her. Once I knew how her presence there gave me a sense of being, I could not un-know it.

"He'll come to you, Maveen," I said, feeling in my heart that it would be so.

After that topic died, we simply sat and listened to the featured Porter music.

"I love that song Vaughn Monroe sings," Maveen said, closing her eyes as Keely Smith oozed "What is This Thing Called Love."

I stopped humming along long enough to comment. "The one Farmer Gray plays, 'Ghost Riders In the Sky'?"

"Yeah. That's it. It's not really country, is it?"

"Nope. Neither is 'Mockingbird Hill'. Not totally. Patti Page is mostly a pop singer. But Farmer Gray plays that song, too. So, over all, I'm not too bad off. It's when all I hear is bluegrass all day long that I get – sorta addle-brained, you know?"

The little timer went off, and I tried to figure out how to pull out the hot pans without scorching myself. After all, I wasn't exactly experienced. So Maveen guided me through the intricate process. We carefully turned the layers out on waxed papered plates to set into the refrigerator for a quick cool.

As they cooled, we sat quietly through several more tunes, some familiar, others not as much. But all lovely and Porter-y. We hummed along and sang with the ones we knew, comfortable as two old shoes together, checking the cake layers periodically until they were ready to ice.

"What color do you want the frosting?" Maveen asked, pointing to a little box with tiny bottles of assorted colors.

"Can I do any I like?"

"Shoot, yeah," she grinned. I picked the blue and dribbled several drops into the creamy batch I'd already begun mixing. As I turned the mixer on high and watched, soft yellow and blue turned a lovely shade of pale sea green.

"Ooo, look at it," I exulted, thrilled beyond words at my wonderful creation. My excitement grew as I spread the concoction over and around the first cake tier.

"It's real, real pretty," Maveen cooed as she placed the second layer atop the first and I began to ice it. She showed me how to smooth and fill in the creases. By the third layer I was slapping it on like the mad scientist. I even made the frosting curl like ocean waves by flapping the spatula against the sea of aquamarine.

"What's wrong with your hand?" Maveen asked, peering at the reddish rash on my hands that had begun appearing right after we'd gone to the farm. "What is that? Does it hurt?"

"No. It itches sometimes." I shrugged. "Don't know what it is. Mama's gonna take me to Dr. Wright soon's I get back home for good. He's not ever open when I'm home on the weekend." Since the rash didn't hurt, I wasn't too conscious of it.

"Look at you," Maveen crowed as I licked the mixer blades clean and gazed in awe at the tall, festive cake. "You are a cook now," she gushed and hugged me hugely.

Just then, Nat King Cole belted out Porter's "Just One of Those Things." "He's Daddy's favorite crooner," I declared, dancing around as I helped Maveen clear the table and wash up the cake pans, bowls and utensils.

Then we sat down and ate a slice of the cake. "Just a small one," Maveen insisted as I started to cut hers. "I licked some of the batter and frosting, too," she reminded me.

"Yeah," I agreed and cut us two slim pieces. We sat at the red-topped, chrome-wrapped table and ate to Bing Crosby's rendition of "You Do Something To Me."

"Mm," Maveen groaned with pleasure. "This is *good*, Sadie."

"Yeah," I agreed, pride swelling. "Wish I was hungrier, though. Licking the bowls and spatula filled me up." I finished my small portion and put the lid on the cake, proud as punch over my masterpiece.

Later, Mama and Daddy came in and enjoyed a slice, too, bragging like I'd won the Academy Award. I loved it. "I wish Maveen could babysit us all the time," I said to Mama as we washed and rinsed their desert plates. I did drying duty and put them away.

"We already thought of that," Mama said. "She's gotta take care of her mama during the day when we need somebody here. She'd really like to, but I think she's too broken up right now over being separated from Gene to handle a full-time job taking care of kids."

"Yeah." Oh, but how I'd love to be with Maveen and be home, too.

"Just you wait and see. It won't be long before we figure out a way for you to stay home." Mama hugged me and kissed the top of my head. When I didn't respond, she said brightly, "Say, why don't you take the rest of the cake to Grandma's. She's just got to see what you've done all on your own. I'll bet they'll all love it."

I sighed and nodded. "Okay." Maybe they would. I just hated the thought of leaving home again.

⌘ ⌘ ⌘ ⌘ ⌘ ⌘ ⌘

"She baked it all by herself," Mama gushed to the Melton family at large. It was just past suppertime when we got there. Daddy toted the cake carrier in and placed it on the new chest-type freezer that sat along one kitchen wall. Grandma's decision to buy it on time came after she gleaned three more families' weekly laundry. The salary increase allowed the purchase. Grandma said – in so many words – that it would revolutionize her canning and such. She wouldn't have to worry about foods spoiling.

Today, my colorful cake looked mighty pretty setting there atop it.

Nellie Jane looked impressed enough. Grandma nodded. The noncommittal kind. Empty face. Guarded body language. "It's real good," Mama added and looked at me with pride. Then she looked at Grandma. "Don't you want to try a piece, Mrs. Melton?"

My grandmother started shaking her head slowly back and forth. "I don't eat anything green," she said matter-of-factly.

"But it's just food coloring," Mama said gently. She loved my Grandma like her own mama and usually she could coax her into anything reasonable.

"No," Grandma insisted. "I'm scared of anything green going in my belly."

"S'okay," I muttered to Mama, by now feeling something stirring in my chest, a heavy, slushing, icy sensation that moved all over me. Never mind that Nellie Jane smiled approvingly and that the boys all stood around like football tackles waiting for the whistle. *Grandma didn't want to eat my cake.*

Mama's face emptied and she quickly readied to leave. Her robin's egg blue eyes were all black pupil as she ushered me ahead of her out the screen door.

"Walk me to the car, honey," she whispered. As we spanned the neatly swept yard to the parking lot, silently passing Grandpa holding court with visiting kin, she put her arm snuggly around me. "Don't mind her, darlin'. She's funny about some things, is all." But there was little conviction behind her words and I heard, *felt* a touch of something alien to my mother: offense.

Tears pushed so insistently against my throat and behind my eyes that I clenched my teeth together to stem them. It didn't help. The darned things came splashing over and ran down my face like spring water tumbling over a rocky bed.

Behind the car, Mama pulled me into her arms and held me, shielding me from view. With my face pressed into her neck and inhaling her Avon Cotillion fragrance and Ponds face powder, I cried softly, deeply as I'd never done. It wasn't like my dragon-breathing kind of tantrum. It was different. Deep. Consuming. Heavy.

Her round softness welcomed me, gave me temporary haven. Soothed.

When the tears ceased, I drew myself up and said, "I'll be okay, Mama."

She looked deeply into my eyes, her soul shining through, connecting with mine. "I know," she said gently. "My little girl's growing up."

"We'll get you home soon," she said, smiling softly.

She and Daddy left shortly thereafter. I stood rooted there, my heart following them as the ancient Ford chugged up the long dirt road. I remained there until it disappeared over the crest into the dusky evening and the sound was no more. I heard instead the easy, random talk of kin from the front yard, where the single light bulb now limned them as they burst into laughter during one of Grandpa's yarns.

Head down, plodding silently on bare feet, I leaned into the encroaching darkness that circled the happy stage and rapt audience that was Grandpa's. Tonight being Sunday, no one shelled peas or broke string beans. But I didn't want to talk with anyone. With Grandpa's tale revving up, no one noticed me as I slipped through the screen door into the empty house. It was dark. And I was glad.

Yet – the silence rang loudly.

The emptiness of the house washed over me. Cried out. I tried to shut it out, but it was too persistent. My chest began to take on the heaviness of cold, wet concrete again. I peered around in the darkness for a place to be and realized that, for the first time ever, I felt a grown-up anger.

I went to the pallet laid in an out-of-the-way corner, already occupied by my little sleeping brother, curled up with my arm thrown protectively over him and soon, fell into a deep, restless slumber.

⌘ ⌘ ⌘ ⌘ ⌘ ⌘ ⌘

All week long, I lay around when I wasn't helping with chores. The empty space left by Maveen howled and groaned. Grandma seemed not to miss a lick with her own chores agenda, though I suspected that Gene's distancing and simmering anger was beginning to wear her thin.

I spent much solitude in the meadow on pretty days, thinking about home, where peace and kindness abounded.

I thought of Maveen, at her mama's house so close to ours, and suddenly, I wanted to go home so badly I hurt all inside. My tummy ached again and my head throbbed. The next morning, I saw blood stains on the pallet and in my panties. This time, Grandma saw and wordlessly supplied me with pads, homemade but reliable.

Neediness assailed me. I instinctively cringed from the feeling. I wanted to dive into a hole and pull it in after me to cover my shame of the ghastly craving. It just wasn't there for me, the validation and succor for which my very pores screamed and wailed.

Even Frances, when I helped slop her, ignored me.

"Why don't Grandma love me?" I asked Nellie Jane that evening as we lolled in the woods, sampling the first of the muscadines and scuppernongs.

"Why do you think that?" She seemed truly confused.

"I don't know," I spit out the seeds of the still tangy pulp. The purple fruit, so like Concord grapes, was not yet completely ripe. "She just don't act like she does sometimes."

Nellie Jane didn't say anything else. But the next day, as we took a walk, she said, "I told Ma you didn't think she loved you. And she said, 'Why does Sadie think that? She ought to know that I love her.'"

The words warmed me a bit, but I wondered at the same time why Grandma herself had not reassured me?

Melancholy stirred inside me like thick sugarcane syrup, the kind Grandpa bought in gallon buckets to feed the fruit of his loins. King's Golden Syrup. We used tin plates in which – atop the wooden stove – to melt scoops of freshly churned butter, covered it with the golden syrup, stirred it together over heat and sopped it with fluffy, hot buttermilk biscuits.

The flavor that day was buttery-caramel. A bittersweet blend of missing home and designing my escape.

A blueprint commenced to form in my brain. On Wednesday, I watched all the adults scatter to their separate chores, older males down to the back bottoms and Grandma to the barn to gather eggs. When Clarence Henry and Doodle-Bug, visiting again, disappeared into the woods to explore, I saw my chance and grabbed Little Joe's hand.

"C'mon," I whispered to him, tugging his hand.

He gazed up trustingly at me with huge, bottomless blue eyes as he toddled along beside me, trying to keep up with my longer stride. We had to hurry. Grandma wouldn't be at the barn very long. Nellie Jane ironed clothes inside the house, immersed in her favorite radio soap opera, "Our Gal Sunday."

Little Joe and I moved quickly up the dirt road that converged into the paved highway, just past the corn patch. The high stalks soon shielded us from view of the farm. I knew that once we spanned the hill and passed the Donalds' place at the end of our road, the chance of our being spotted grew slimmer.

We were going home.

It wasn't that far because we drove the distance home every Saturday and then back again each Sunday evening on our return. We passed mostly farms. I was familiar with the turn-offs, the main one leading down into the mill village. The map lodged in my mind, clear as morning dew.

Little Joe compliantly hung onto my hand as we passed the Donalds' small dwelling, where Mr. and Mrs. Donalds rested in the shade of their porch. I rushed past without looking at them and turned up the main road.

Soon, Little Joe and I passed the Berry farm. In the distance, I saw Mr. Berry, straw hat hung low over his forehead, plowing up dead bean stalks. Long stretches of fields moved past as I picked up my stride, forcing Little Joe into an uneven trot. He almost stumbled several times, forcing me to slow down.

We passed more fields and farmhouses and I saw a turn-off bordered by a colored church and a country store. No turn here. I wiped sweat off my forehead.

"You okay, Little Joe?" I asked. He looked weary.

"Huh uh. I tired. Where we goin'?" he asked, eyes unfailingly trusting.

"Home. Try to keep going, okay? It's not much farther."

I aimed my stride straight ahead because I knew the next turnoff, still several miles away, would be into our village.

The day was sunny but not as hot as usual for late August. As the sun began to give way to dusk, a soft cooling breeze occasionally ruffled my sweat-dampened hair. The momentum built inside me, like a rising, bubbling creek of sweet cool water.

Home. Mama. Daddy. Maveen.

Then I heard it.

Chugga lugga lugga.

Instinctively, protectively, I pulled Little Joe from the rough pavement onto the road's dirt shoulder. I turned to look in the direction of the approaching vehicle.

It was Grandpa's truck. Oh no.

So close…so close to home. Oh no, God. Not now.

The battered old black truck rattled to a halt, engine coughing and burping as it idled. Grandpa, eyes set straight ahead, muttered in a cool flat voice, "Get in."

We clamored aboard. Wordlessly, Grandpa turned the truck around and *chugalugged* back down the road. The silent trip ended a while later when we lumbered down the dirt road and chugged to a halt in the dirt parking lot.

Grandma met me at the front door with the biggest hickory stick I'd ever seen. Without a word she took me into the bedroom and began to whap me with her weapon. Actually, I felt little pain, so numb was I with disappointment.

And embarrassment, a new thing with me. Alien. Frustrating.

I worked up a few tears, just to validate the punishment, but when I walked out of that bedroom and past Nellie Jane, her expression was one of amusement. At least, that's the way I read it. When I scowled at her, she sorta – smirked.

Anger rose up in me. The injustice singed me. My escape being aborted and the beating all added up to a humongous dose of aggravation. I began to do the dragon-breathing thing and exploded.

"It didn't hurt!" I shrieked at Nellie Jane.

Her grin grew wider. "Mama?" she sing-songed. "Sadie said it didn't hurt."

Grandma appeared, nose a'flare. "Oh, she did, did she? Well, come 'ere, girl. We'll see what hurt is." She yanked me back into the bedroom for another whaling.

That time, my tears were real. And my trust in Nellie Jane dropped dramatically. And again, more dramatically than ever, placelessness swallowed me whole.

chapter seven

*"And then the day came, when the risk it took to remain tight in the bud
was more painful than the risk it took to blossom."*
Anias Nin

In retrospect, I knew that I'd done wrong, disappearing like that with Little Joe. My grandparents had spent frantic hours looking all over the farm for us. Not until they asked the Donalds if they'd seen two kids were they enlightened. The elderly couple had pointed them in our direction.

"Sadie, they was worried half to death," Nellie Jane confided later that day. "And I was, too. Didn't you stop and think how we'd feel when you just up and disappeared? Why, anything coulda happened to you. With ol' Bill Chancy living across the woods, ya'll coulda been snatched by him." Chancy had been questioned and released in a local rape-murder case several years back. The stigma continued to trail him like black smoke.

I shrugged, eaten alive with guilt by now. "Why did you laugh when I got a whupping?" I asked, hurt, needing to understand.

Nellie Jane just looked at me strangely for a long moment. "Sometimes – when things are really, really bad, I don't know how to act. So I end up grinning like a possum. I try not to, but I feel that grin just stretching over my face. I just can't help it." She shrugged limply. "Stupid, ain't it? And mean." She looked so sad I nearly cried. My emotions were like up in a whirlwind one moment and plunging over the Mill River dam the next.

"Yeah. It really made me mad when you laughed at me."

"Wad'n at you. And I'm sorry."

I knew then that it was not at me. Somehow, mystically, I understood Nellie Jane's complex psyche, one that, at times, failed to distinguish between love and hate, loyalty and betrayal. But in her, love and loyalty always, eventually, won out. That was the important thing.

"S'okay," I murmured and we hugged each other in mutual forgiveness.

⌘ ⌘ ⌘ ⌘ ⌘ ⌘ ⌘

Grandma wasn't quite as quick to show mercy. I still had to own my sin.

"Just wait till I tell your Mama and Daddy what you done," Grandma had told me right after the dirty deed of my running off. Now, I faced that confrontation with fear and trepidation. Not that Mama and Daddy were ever, ever mean. But they were really big on doing the right thing and I had not done the right thing by running away.

Guilt pulled heavily at me, like I alone dragged Grandpa's steel-bladed plow through hard, rocky terrain. Each time I looked back upon it, the black transgression appeared more and more revolting.

The week seemed interminable as I waited for the axe to drop. Cousin Doodle-Bug was dropped off for yet another visit, but I ignored him. He no longer seemed as inclined to pester me after the thrashing he'd gotten from Grandma on his last visit.

I spent lots of solitary time in the meadow. Thinking on what I'd done. Thinking on how I'd really *done myself in.* One day, I ventured into my favorite barn stall. I lay on the hay-carpet and reminisced about the summer, missing home and

Maveen more than ever. I thought how Gene had up and moved out the day before my caper.

"I love Maveen, Ma. She's my wife and I'm going to her. We'll get a Mill Hill house in a few days. But in the meantime, I'm going to be with her."

He'd packed his bag and left faster'n you could say, "Scat." I was happy for Maveen, knowing how crazy she was about Gene, and I was proud of him for standing up for her. I decided then and there that when I married, I wanted to marry somebody who would always put me first. Like Gene did Maveen and Daddy did Mama.

Today, I felt my bladder throb and went to the only barn stall with a door. There, I climbed up on the rustic, smelly toilet seat, squatted, and just as I began to relieve myself through the less-than-sanitary hole, I heard something.

About the same time I smelled cigarette smoke

A snicker? Then another. A definite sniggering laugh. More than one.

I promptly finished and jumped down from the perch. I heard the scuttle of retreating footsteps and rushed to discover the identity of the interlopers. Doodle-Bug and Clarence Henry, by now at a safe distance, turned around, hooting and howling, springing up and down like goofy jumping-jacks, hollering, "We seen you! We seen you!"

They'd been peeping through the bottom missing slat on the toilet stall as I did my private duty. I should 'a known it was them because they were always sneaking around behind the barn smoking Gene's Camel cigarette butts.

Anger and embarrassment warred.

Anger won, evoking my dragon-breathing, teeth-clenched eruption, this time no Puff the Magic Dragon.

"*I Hope God strikes you blind you ol' blackguards!*" I shrieked, not sure exactly of the name's origin but knowing that it meant somebody was the lowest of the low. It was a term Grandma used when especially inflamed at somebody.

"Stupid ol' *Lamaar!*" I tacked on for good measure, almost hoping for a fight with Doodle. I felt that I could, in that moment, snatch up a rock or a hoe or something to whale the daylights out of 'im.

Undeterred, they disappeared over the hill, still howling with laughter.

I strolled limply down to Frances' pen and found her napping as usual. I sighed and returned to my stall-haven where its silence swallowed up my sense of violation. I settled into and soaked up its peace and quiet. I found myself wishing more than ever for home and hearth.

A soft rustling caught my attention. From the opposite wall of my stall, I saw the hay divide as a copper-colored snake glided territorially from beneath the heap and then move again beneath the fragrant cover. The rustle of straw continued, but I could no longer see it.

Shock coursed through me.

Snake!

Run!

I was on my feet and scurrying away before the import struck me fully. "Grandma!" I ran into the house yelling. "Grandma! There's a snake down there."

Grandma was out the door following me, pretty well keeping astride as we cautiously approached the vicinity where I'd last seen the slimy intruder.

"Right there," I pointed from a safe distance. She snatched a hoe from the wall hook and commenced to slowly, cautiously part the straw with the implement's sharp metal blade. "There it is," she muttered.

I turned away, covering my face with both hands. I shuddered as, moments later, I looked over my shoulder when

Grandma displayed the headless serpent, now hung lifelessly over the hoe's blade. It was about five-feet in length with intricate coppery and tan markings. Beautiful. Hypnotically so, like a great cheetah.

She looked at me, her eyes somber, concerned. "It's a copperhead, Sadie. It was providential that you seen it when you did. It coulda bit you 'fore you knowed what happened. You coulda been killed." She moved outside to hang the reptile over the barbed wire fence, muttering, "Thank the good Lord."

And I knew in that moment.

Grandma loved me.

⌘ ⌘ ⌘ ⌘ ⌘ ⌘ ⌘

Loved me, she did. But that still didn't keep her from informing Daddy and Mama of my dastardly deed. I knew she would, because she told me so. I knew that, to Grandma's way of thinking, something so serious as running away warranted extra accountability from the guilty.

Little Joe, of course, was an innocent bystander. This drama, my flighty abandonment of sensible behavior, had been told and retold at every opportunity, at least four or five times a day. Every time I heard it, I felt more vile and contemptible. A mere worm. Even Nellie Jane seemed to avoid me.

The lowest was when Clarence Henry and Doodle-Bug shunned me.

I wasn't even worthy of ridicule.

Grandpa Melton, great storyteller that he was, could not resist the temptation to embellish a bit. "If I hadn't a come along when I did, Sadie was a'headin' em' off past that church and store. Why, they'd a ended up no tellin' where."

That depiction turned my mouth inside out like a persimmon before frost. I wanted to scream that I did so know where

I was going and had no intention of taking the wrong turnoff, but I bit my tongue, allowing Grandpa his moment of glory and also realizing I was already in deep enough crap without calling poor ol' Grandpa a liar.

Saturday arrived. My folks would come to collect my little brother and me early in the day. I awoke before anyone stirred. Before even Old Red crowed.

I picked over my grits and bypassed the caramel-y concoction of butter and golden syrup. I slipped out the front screen door unnoticed and crept around to the back of the house.

Usually, on Saturdays, anticipation made my pulse leap and my feet restless. I would hover in the parking lot, eagerly watching for our old car to crest the hill and noisily lumber its way toward me. When it chugged to a stop I would yank open the door and throw myself into Mama's arms before she could even swing her legs to the side and slide her feet to the ground. After a long, fierce hug, I'd dash around and greet Daddy the same way.

Not this time. Today, I hid in the backyard, amongst Grandma's flower bushes. After what seemed an eternity, I heard my parents' noisy, chugging engine when it arrived and died. I heard the car doors open and, moments later, slam shut. Then quiet prevailed.

With my back firmly pressed to the weathered, paint-less exterior house wall, I perched there, knobby knees drawn to chest, as still as a feline-stalked mockingbird. Time stretched out and the damp, red clay-dirt grew hard under my bony fanny. I squirmed and shifted my bottom.

"Sadie?"

I jolted at the sound. *Mama. It was Mama's voice.*

She didn't come around the corner but she knew. Somehow, she knew where I was.

And why.

"Honey, come on out," she said gently. "Daddy and I ain't mad at you."

Not mad? My heart began to stir and flounder upward from the black pit of despair and guilt. Shame.

I slowly stood, quivery legs stiff from the long, cramped position, then hesitantly crept to the corner and peered around it. Mama was not there. She'd apparently gone back inside to collect Little Joe because Daddy was already walking toward the car, whistling.

Whistling?

Daddy sure didn't sound mad. Nor did he look mad when he glanced over his shoulder and caught me peeking around the corner. My breath hitched for a heartbeat, dread stirring. After all, Daddy wasn't always as quickly forgiving as Mama. His full mouth curled up at one corner. Then he winked at me and jerked his head in the direction of the car, a wordless *let's go.* Mama appeared with Little Joe in tow. I began to walk in their direction, my heart daring to begin to hope…just a little.

I quickly climbed into the tattered old back seat beside Little Joe, who grinned happily up at me, obviously blissful to see Mama and Daddy. Feeling as contrite as I'd ever felt in my life, I clasped my hands together and waited, resigned to my fate.

Mama looked over her shoulder at me and smiled. "Daddy and I figure you learned your lesson when Grandma Melton whupped you." She reached over the seat and took my hand. "What you did was wrong. It really scared everybody. But we understand why you did what you did."

"We do, Sadie," Daddy said in a husky way.

I swiped a tear from my cheek and snuffled. "I'm sorry," I whispered.

"We know you are." Then she smiled softly at me as only your mama can, like the love starts at her toes and gushes up and spills out her beautiful cornflower blue eyes to splash all over you. You can go swimming in it and float on top of it. It lifts you to the sky and soars you above dark clouds.

Into lemony sunshine.

"Let's go home, Sadie," she said softly. "This time for good."

epilogue

True to their word, my parents never farmed us out to Grandma again. Nor to anyone else, for that matter. We never again, until we married, left hearth and home.

But we did continue to visit Grandma's farm each Sunday.

Two weeks after we went home, Mama and Daddy brought Little Joe and me down to the farm for our weekly visit. It was later than usual and we smelled supper cooking when we got out of the car.

"Mmm," Mama said. "Smells like ham."

"Or sausage," Daddy added. "Maybe we'll get some."

Excited, I ran down across the yard, past Grandpa and on down the slope to Frances' pen. When I ground to a halt there, the silence was eerie.

The pen was empty.

I ran back to the house just as the family sat down to supper. The table was laden with delicious fare. Fluffy biscuits, fried ham and red gravy, golden buttery grits, sausage and scrambled eggs. My stomach began to rumble as I took my place behind the table. Room had been made for Mama and Daddy across from me.

Nellie Jane sat beside me, unusually silent. Pale. She watched me with this strange look on her face.

"What?" I whispered.

"Shh," Mama said, motioning toward Grandma, who was about to say the blessing.

"Lord, bless this food of which we are about to partake. Use it to the nourishment of our body. Amen."

Tonight, the boys skipped their show, in deference to Mama and Daddy's presence. *What a relief*, I thought.

Then I remembered. "Nellie Jane," I whispered, "where's Frances?"

She looked at me for a long time, sadness heavy in her gaze. Then she nodded to the platter of sausage and the bowl of ham and red-eye gravy.

"There's Frances," she said, puckering and quickly sniffing back tears.

Neither of us ate a bite that night.

⌘ ⌘ ⌘ ⌘ ⌘ ⌘ ⌘

Weekly, Nellie Jane and I would disappear to the meadow or woods to catch up and share our lives, our dreams. Yeah, Nellie Jane had them just like I did. Not as grandiose as mine, but she still had dreams, like marrying Billy, a man she'd begun courting in her sixteenth year.

One Indian Summer day in the fall of our home-going, while in the meadow lounging on a blanket, Nellie Jane told me about the revival that'd just ended at the Methodist Church.

"Sadie, that pot-bellied preacher was the most fearsome thing I'd ever seen," she insisted, the most animated I'd ever seen her. Delicious anticipation swirled inside me as I raptly waited for the rest of the story.

"He preached like his shirt tail was on fire and told about how if we don't confess our sins, we'll all be cast into the lake of fire that burns forever and ever. Well, Doodle and Clarence Henry was sittin' on the front pew, next to me. I watched 'em as their eyes got bigger and bigger and then that preacher man started rattlin' off all them who would be lost. He went down the list and when he got to the place the Bible says that all liars would be cast into that lake that burns forever, they started cryin' like babies."

I clapped my hands over my mouth, stifling giggles, and then thought better of it. This was serious, this eternity thing. "What happened?"

She grinned from ear to ear, a beautiful sight on Nellie Jane. "When he give 'at altar call, I thought Doodle and Clarence Henry was gonna knock each other down runnin' to that altar to pray for forgiveness of their sins."

Then, I lost the battle and burst into laughter with Nellie Jane echoing. "How are they doing now they got religion?" I asked when my laughter died down.

Nellie Jane sobered. "Well, actually, Sadie, they're doing pretty good. For them, I mean." She cut her eyes at me, as in *wait and see*. Then silence settled over us, comfortable and good, and memories of the summer began to float through my mind. Suddenly, like a Jack-in-the–box, the day Grandma rejected my cake popped up. I felt anew the mortification. The hurt.

I took the plunge and asked her, "Nellie Jane, why wouldn't Grandma eat my cake?" My heart began to hammer and my breath grew short, but I wanted to know.

She looked at me as a blush crawled slowly up her pale neck. I felt her embarrassment and was sorry that I'd asked. I was about to apologize when she replied, "Sadie, Ma's funny about food. She was telling the truth about being afraid to eat anything green. Comes from when food spoils and turns green-ish, you know? And – remember you had a bad rash on your hands that summer?"

"Yeah."

"Well, she was as afraid of germs as she was of spoilt food. She just didn't want you to spread germs by handling the food."

The flash of fresh hurt was mild, as was my defensive reply. "Dr. Wright said it was an allergy. Called it eczema, I think.

Something on the farm was causing it because it went away for good when I went home. It wasn't a germ thing."

Nellie Jane looked at me sympathetically. "Just try tellin' Ma that." Then she laughed softly. "She's just set in her ways, Sadie. And by the way, I loved your cake. And so did the boys."

I burst into laughter. "Yeah. I remember. That cake disappeared faster'n you could say booger-boo. Thanks for the compliment."

"You're welcome," she said, that beautiful shyness creeping back into her voice.

"Love you, Nellie Jane," I said.

"Love you, too," she said, blushing pinker than ever and returning my smile.

We've remained close through the years. No closer friend have I had than my Aunt Nellie Jane, who found happiness and a beautiful family with her Billy.

Nellie Jane was a late bloomer, too. Fortunately, marriage and motherhood agreed with her. She grew prettier with time. And more confident. Like the other Melton women, she's battled weight all through the years. Most of the time, she wins. Overall, she's happy just to maintain a healthy level.

Me? I've fluffed up to a healthy size. Being an overachiever, I refuse to *let myself go*, as Grandma Melton used to say. So, if I gain three to five pounds over my ideal one-hundred-thirty, I stop the world, go hungry, lose it, then get on with life.

"You're obsessive," my own daughter Kaleigh sometimes tells me. But she grins when she says it, knowing that that's *me*. I *am* obsessive. But it's the good kind.

Maveen? Well, she and Gene had three beautiful daughters and have grown old together, enjoying grandchildren and family reunions that she, Nellie Jane and I organize. She's still beautiful. Her gray hair is dyed auburn and she's still thin as a rail, giving her a girlish look even all these years later.

As always, she looks gorgeous in anything she wears, and those deep-set silvery eyes still radiate love and generosity. One thing Maveen did that thrilled me was to go back to school and get her GED credits. She'd dropped out of school in the eighth grade, a common occurrence in those days.

By the time her own Annie Ruth was in eighth grade, Maveen told me one day, "I don't want my kids to be smarter'n me. It was okay for you to be smarter, Sadie, but my own kids?" She shook her head decisively. "Huh uh."

Nellie Jane and I laughed along with her, as at ease with each other as we'd been all those years back when we'd lounged in the meadow beneath blue southern sky, watching frothy white clouds float overhead. This day, however, we sat on Maveen's bed, crosslegged and sipping gourmet coffee. The bedspread was not hobnail but Laura Ashley. Gene, like my dad, went back to night school, upgraded his education and became my father's business partner in Melton's Heating and Air Conditioning.

Maveen now wore the best in clothing. She lived in a luxurious two-story, four-thousand-square-foot brick structure, in a nice neighborhood.

"My, my," I said, holding up my Starbucks cup, "our tastes have gotten fancy along the way."

"Yeah," Maveen laughed. "You oughta buy for my kids. You'd really *know fancy.*" Then she grew contemplative. "I'm really happy with my life. Ya'll know that. It's just − the thing I really hate that I done was drop out of school. Sometimes, I think the kids are ashamed of me when I meet their friends' parents here in this neighborhood. All them got college educations. Speak better'n me. Y'know?" She shrugged limply, sighed and raised her eyebrows. "But that's all water under the bridge, huh? Too late to turn back now, as the song goes." She forced a smile.

"I know I'm one to talk, Maveen," Nellie Jane said, "but you can start by going to the Anderson night school and get your high school diploma."

"That's right, Maveen," I jumped in. "It's never too late. I read about a woman who finished college in her nineties. The best part of the story is that she was loved by everybody on campus. During my college years, I met quite a few midlife students. Hey," I playfully poked her shoulder. "If anybody can do it, you can."

"You think?" Maveen perked up, eyes sparkling with anticipation. "You really think I could do it, Sadie?"

"Shoot yeah."

"*Gol-lay* – I'd really love to do that."

"And Maveen," I injected, "your girls aren't ashamed of you. Never. You should hear what they say when you're not around. They compare you to their friends' moms and say how their mama is always there for them, not out at club meetings or working at careers. They brag about how you're always the first to volunteer to bake cookies and cakes for good causes and how your cooking is the best in the world. Most of all, they say how you love and protect them. I love to hear them say how you keep them in line by saying, 'You're big, but I'm bigger. I can still whup your butt.'" We all three broke into laughter then. "Like Nellie Jane, you're first and foremost a mama. And wife. Now, it's time to be you."

Maveen took that in, her eyes running a range of emotions from pride to humility, growing more and more moist. "So," I added, "When you go back to school, it will be something you do for yourself. The world will open up to you. You'll meet interesting people and begin to tune into their world of knowledge. Your boundaries will enlarge. You'll discover literature and science and art and other things you've never tasted of."

I smiled at her, my heart singing. "Maveen, you'll love it."

We turned the conversation to the upcoming family reunion. "Let's get Clarence Henry to do the devotional," I suggested. We had several ministers in the clan now so we tried to rotate the honor of the invocation delivery. Clarence Henry's religion had "took" and he'd served in the Methodist church for decades now.

"We'll miss Doodle-Bug," Maveen sighed. "He's the fourth to die in a car wreck, ain't he?"

I nodded. "Uncle Bill and his wife Lillian – that was a real shock. Still miss them after all these years."

Nellie Jane rolled her eyes and declared, "Well, I won't ever accept that it's a Melton curse, the car wrecks. More likely just bad driving."

"We don't have to accept it either way. Some things just happen," I said. "Let's lighten up, girls. Life's hard enough as it is without making it worse with such notions."

So Maveen signed up for night school that very next semester. Her enthusiasm stirred up Nellie Jane's interest in some of the English coursebooks and the two of them would share and collaborate on Maveen's theme papers. Nellie Jane found that she had a natural grasp of literature and English. Unlike me, she was pretty good with numbers, too.

Next semester, Nellie Jane began night classes, too. Both she and Maveen finished high school with flying colors. And much pride. Needless to say, the three of us had many more interesting topics to explore afterward.

Yet, the essence of *us* remained unchanged.

History and blood and unconditional love forever link and identify us.

After that, time, life and experience seasoned and mellowed us into an even better *us*.

The Melton family tree and its branches now sport teachers, pastors, doctors, dentists, medical professionals, musicians, artists and authors. Other respectful professions knit these together in an impressive collage of honor and dignity.

More and more, I learned to appreciate Grandma Melton's strengths and stoicism as I later faced my own battles in this arena called life. I learned that – considering her near pauper existence, temperament, cultural and educational limitations – Grandma actually did quite well.

In the late sixties, Grandma's chest-fluttering was diagnosed as heart failure. Medication kept her going, even six months beyond Grandpa's sudden demise. When her "honey" passed, Grandma was never the same, and I realized anew the intimacy of their union. The love there, punctuated through the years by soft-spoken "honeys" and "darlins," and the impeccable respect that through the poverty and bedlam, at times, had seamlessly glued it all together.

Now, her loss was almost unbearable. No amount of coaxing drew her out of her grief. When Daddy pleaded with her to please not torture herself, she looked at him sadly, heart in eyes and murmured, "I can't help it, Joe."

Maveen insisted upon moving my invalid Grandma into Maveen's comfortable home, prepared with her very own private suite and cable television, and took care of her mother-in-law, loving and nurturing her in her last days. Grandma, in turn, unleashed her love upon Maveen. The peace was complete. It was totally beautiful.

In the months following my home-going that year, I found myself looking back on who I was before that transforming summer. It was difficult because so much that happened that season flavored my world differently from anything I'd ever tasted or whiffed.

But the lemony flavor came back to me, as fresh and tangy as ever and I could still remember that girl, the one who could not bear anyone being sad. So she often took upon her small shoulders the responsibility of keeping family and friends happy. Her friends were – well, heck, *everybody.*

I knew this girl intimately because she lived inside me, weaving dreams and quickening the me who believed with all my heart in Santa Claus, the Tooth Fairy and the Easter Bunny. In childhood, we sang the same melody and finished each other's sentences and thoughts.

Our sighs, induced by a kind word, rode out in unison.

The lemony-vanilla contentment of those years remains, even now, indelible.

Mmm. I can still smell the vanilla fragrance of Alma Rock's kitchen when she made vanilla custard pie every Wednesday. Alma, Maveen's mama, was my neighbor. And friend. And at that time in my life, she became more than a friend.

Maveen, now happily living in her own mill-village house with Gene, across the river bridge from us, didn't mind sharing her mama with me. Recuperated from her summer ailments, Alma seemed stronger than ever. Two adolescent sons still resided with her, and I knew she didn't have much money for groceries since her husband was the only working member of her household. They were still paying hospital bills and times were tough.

Mama admiringly said that Alma was one of those rare creatures who could take a dollar and stretch it to kingdom come and back. She even foraged ingredients to make a dessert for each day of the week. Sometimes it was a simple rice pudding. Sometimes shortbread.

"C'mon in, Sadie. Pull up a chair and I'll get your custard pie," she'd say as she swung wide her front door in greeting.

Despite the fact that Mama and Daddy had hired another live-in housekeeper/cook, Alma's house became my refuge while they worked the mill's second shift. Millie, our new babysitter was nice and we got along fine, but she wasn't Alma. Alma filled some emotional vacuum inside me, and right then, that's what I needed.

Daddy's vigilance of his offspring lightened up that year. I think Mama played a part in opening him up to the changes in me, the needs. Everything about him softened. He loved me as intensely and was still protective. Only difference was that now he seemed to venture into my world, discerning my need to move about and have different experiences and influences in my life.

Somehow, he sensed that Alma filled a critical void at just that time.

I grew to anticipate Wednesdays at Alma's house because I knew I'd get a dish of vanilla custard pie. Most of the time, I would go back for seconds.

My thirteenth birthday came and went with a big birthday cake and presents from Mama, Daddy, Maveen and Alma. One Wednesday, I rushed to Alma's house and – anticipation palpable – plopped down at her kitchen table.

But this time, something was different. Off-kilter.

Today, Alma's mind seemed somewhere else entirely. The pie sat in its niche on the counter, but she didn't smile and dish up my dessert as usual. Rather, she went about her chores in a studied way that told me she wasn't going to share with me this time.

After a while, she said absently, "You'd better go on home now, honey. I'm not really feeling well."

It was so alien, being downright dismissed by Alma, that I shuffled my bare feet and awkwardly hovered in the kitchen doorway like a puppy waiting for a scrap of food. She put her broom away and went silently to her room and shut the door softly behind her.

I went home, dragging my proverbial tail behind me.

A huge lump swelled in my throat and I knew in that moment that I had somehow abused her generosity. After the summer at the farm, I'd been forced to reevaluate many things about myself.

I faced another epiphany.

Truth was, at times I was self-serving. I'd taken Alma's generosity for granted, demanding second helpings when she had three lumbering, hollow-legged males to fill up. Because of medical bills, her lifestyle had plummeted that summer. And wearing adolescent "what-about-me?" blinders, I'd overshot my demands. I cringed now at my expectations of Alma. She loved me, true, but she was poor, with a family to feed, something I had not considered when asking for seconds on the pie.

It grieved me that I had, with a child's simple trust, taken her for granted. I had made her sad.

That epiphany birthed another change in my direction. I didn't know it then, but trust – as I knew it – began to reshape. Integrity took root. The girl inside me, the innocent, impetuous one – still whispered each Wednesday, "Ask Alma for some vanilla custard pie." But the wiser me said, "No." I never did again.

Since I'd learned the much-needed lesson, Alma resumed each Wednesday, placing before me a heaping portion of custard pie. Years later, when I asked her about that day, she said, "It had nothing to do with you, Sadie. Something else was goin' on with me. You know, I'd give you the last scrap of food I had."

But I knew even if Alma's behavior that day had not, indeed, been about me, my reaction and perception served to bring about a self-revelation that would forever alter the course of my life.

In the teen years, that inner-gal annoyed me with her incessant groping for acceptance and recognition. She *humiliated me, dadjimmit.* I struggled to hide and camouflage her presence.

Consistency paid off. In later years, she gradually merged with my perception of *me*, only occasionally popping up like a grotesque Betty Boop with smeared makeup. My horrified reaction drove her back time and time again.

Today, she is almost nonexistent. Strangely, that doesn't please me like I thought it would. In fact – get this – I find myself missing her. Yeah. Especially her spontaneity. Hey, all this melancholy junk spawned by aging gets too, too heavy.

And her ability to see past others' flaws and just – love 'em, y'know? Oh, and I miss her childlike abandonment to joy.

I wonder – would she come back? At least when I need her?

In recent days, I've beckoned more and more. Talking and reminiscing. Stuff like that. Because I know that like me, she's a sentimental soul. I know that, even though I put her down so brutally in younger days, she won't turn me away.

More than anything, you see, she loves to make people happy.

Yeah. There were times the aforementioned goulash gave me angst. But it was that helplessness seasoning that hoisted me to another level of awareness. I grew to be mindful that asking too many questions made me a pest and being told to "shut up" was the pits. I learned if I couldn't change things, to ride it out, to cope gracefully. So I curtailed my yakking just to be yakking. That was a big hurdle.

Today, I look back on those marvelous strawberry years, with their sweet-tartness, through a double-sided drama mask, seeing them as wonderfully funny one moment and unbearably tragic the next. Thank God, the boot-camp emotions shifted and changed by the moment.

Thank God, it wasn't forever.

Only puberty could shoot me to Mt. Olympian-ecstasy, thrash me to mortified hash, thrill me to goose-bump pleasure and then plunge me into abject misery, in five minutes flat.

Only adolescence could make me into what I am today. It gave me lifelong friends. It gave me confidence and identity. It gave me role models. It gave me buoyancy.

It gave me....

Me.

If you enjoyed *Flavors*, you can experience more of
Emily Sue Harvey's rare storytelling in:

song of renewal

"An uplifting, heartwarming story of forgiveness,
commitment, and love."
— *New York Times* bestselling author Jill Marie Landis

And in June 2011, discover her newest saga of
strength and redemption:

homefires